"Fred Wah's *Diamond Grill* is a small gem of a book . . . from unpunctuated prose poems, recipes, and excerpts from research materials, to beautifully detailed descriptions of the restaurant itself, funny and warm character sketches, and philosophical musings upon anthropology and identity."

—*Quill & Quire*

". . . a sophisticated and moving text . . . Wah has produced a memorable account . . ."

—*Canadian Literature*

"This collection has been written with delicate precision, and Fred Wah, who takes great care in reproducing his family histories and mixed-race heritage, delicious foods, seasons, and community life, makes the Diamond Grill come alive."

—*Pacific Reader*

"Intimate, moving, funny . . ."

—*Calgary Herald*

". . . Fred Wah's *Diamond Grill* serves up a tasty literary entrée—as well as providing an entrance to a world about which we need to know if we're to understand ourselves."

—*The Vancouver Sun*

"What a joy it is to read his beautifully written sentences, filled to bursting with well chosen language."

—Ruth Raymond

S ELECTED WORKS BY F RED W AH

Faking It: Poetics and Hybridity. Edmonton: NeWest Press, 2000

Alley Alley Home Free. Red Deer: Red Deer College Press, 1992.

So Far. Vancouver: Talonbooks, 1991.

Music at the Heart of Thinking. Red Deer:
Red Deer College Press, 1987.

Waiting for Saskatchewan. Winnipeg: Turnstone Press, 1985.

Grasp The Sparrow's Tail. Kyoto, 1982.

Breathin' My Name With a Sigh. Vancouver: Talonbooks, 1981.

Owners Manual. Lantzville: Island Writing Series, 1981.

Loki is Buried at Smoky Creek: Selected Poetry. Vancouver:
Talonbooks, 1980.

Pictograms from the Interior of B.C. Vancouver: Talonbooks, 197

Earth. Canton, N.Y.: Institute of Further Studies, 1974.

Tree. Vancouver: Vancouver Community Press, 1972.

Among. Toronto: Coach House Press, 1972.

Lardeau. Toronto: Island Press, 1965.

Fred WAH

DIAMOND GRILL

10th ANNIVERSARY

NEWEST PRESS

Library and Archives Canada Cataloguing in Publication

Wah, Fred, 1939-
Diamond Grill / Fred Wah. -- New ed.
(Landmark edition)
First published: 1996.

ISBN-13: 978-1-897126-11-0
ISBN-10: 1-897126-11-5

I. Title. II. Series.
PS8545.A28D52 2006   C813'.54   C2006-903399-4

Board editor: Doug Barbour
Cover and interior design: Val Speidel
Cover photograph: courtesy Fred Wah
Author photograph: Don Denton

NeWest Press acknowledges the support of the Canada Council for
the Arts, the Alberta Foundation for the Arts, and the Edmonton Arts
Council for our publishing program. We also acknowledge the financial
support of the Government of Canada through the Book Publishing
Industry Development Program (BPIDP) for our publishing activities.

NeWest Press
201–8540–109 Street
Edmonton, Alberta T6G 1E6
(780) 432-9427
www.newestpress.com

1 2 3 4 5 09 08 07 06
PRINTED AND BOUND IN CANADA

for Fred, Connie, and Ethel
for family.

You were part Chinese I tell them.
They look at me. I'm pulling their leg.
So I'm Chinese too and that's why my name is Wah.
They don't really believe me. That's o.k.
When you're not "pure" you just make it up.

—from *Waiting for Saskatchewan*

A C K N O W L E D G E M E N T S

A biotext, perhaps more than other literary genres, seems an innately cumulative performance. This one certainly owes its gratitude and occurrence to a great many friends and relatives. bpNichol taunted me to overwrite my fear of the tyranny of prose. My mother has been a generous companion through many long discussions about our family. My cousin Ray Lyons and my brother Don have been unselfish in their willingness to share their affection for our family history and recipes. Nancy Mackenzie and Nicole Markotic encouraged me with their editorial readings of early drafts. Jim Wong-Chu has been gracious with his informed and friendly advice. Pauline Butling has lovingly given much more than merely the first ears and eyes to these texts and our daughters, Jennifer and Erika, have often offered their intelligence and natural curiosity to this project. Aritha van Herk's writerly and intelligent editing plus her friendship and sympathy has resolved and softened, for me, some of the pain and anger behind these stories.

Thanks to the editors of *Intent, Canadian Literature, The Chicago Review, Mixed Messages,* and *Alberta Rebound* for publishing sections of the work in progress. Also, to Ashok Mathur for representing and curating some of the text for the exhibit, *Doors*. Residencies and fellowships from the University of Alberta, Banff Centre for the Arts, and the Calgary Institute for the Humanities all provided time for this project to grow.

After all that, I must take sole responsibility for this text. I wish not to offend any of my family or any of the Chinese Canadians who have known and experienced some of these stories more tangibly than I have. These are not true stories but, rather, poses or postures, necessitated, as I hope is clear in the text, by faking it.

CONTENTS

*I*N THE DIAMOND, AT THE END OF A

long green vinyl aisle between booths of chrome, Naugahyde, and Formica, are two large swinging wooden doors, each with a round hatch of face-sized window. Those kitchen doors can be kicked with such a slap they're heard all the way up to the soda fountain. On the other side of the doors, hardly audible to the customers, echoes a jargon of curses, jokes, and cryptic orders. Stack a hots! Half a dozen fry! Hot beef san! Fingers and tongues all over the place jibe and swear You mucka high!—Thloong you! And outside, running through and around the town, the creeks flow down to the lake with, maybe, a spring thaw. And the prairie sun over the mountains to the east, over my family's shoulders. The journal journey tilts tight-fisted through the gutter of the book, avoiding a place to start—or end. Maps don't have beginnings, just edges. Some frayed and hazy margin of possibility, absence, gap. Shouts in the kitchen. Fish an! Side a fries! Over easy! On brown! I pick up an order and turn, back through the doors, whap! My foot registers more than its own imprint, starts to read the stain of memory.

Thus: a kind of heterocellular recovery reverberates through the busy body, from the foot against that kitchen door on up the leg into the torso and hands, eyes thinking straight ahead, looking through doors and languages, skin recalling its own reconnaissance, cooked into the steamy food, replayed in the folds of elsewhere, always far away, tunneling through the centre of the earth, mouth saying can't forget, mouth saying what I want to know can feed me, what I don't can bleed me.

Mixed Grill is an Entrée at the Diamond

and, as in most Chinese-Canadian restaurants in western Canada, is your typical improvised imitation of Empire cuisine. No kippers or kidney for the Chinese cafe cooks, though. They know the authentic mixed grill alright. It is part of their colonial cook's training, learning to serve the superior race in Hong Kong and Victoria properly, mostly as chefs in private elite clubs and homes. But, as the original lamb chop, split lamb kidney, and pork sausage edges its way onto every small town cafe menu, its ruddy countenance has mutated into something quick and dirty, not grilled at all, but fried.

Shu composes his mixed grill on top of the stove. He throws on a veal chop, a rib-eye, a couple of pork sausages, bacon, and maybe a little piece of liver or a few breaded sweetbreads if he has those left over from the special. While the meat's sizzling he adds a handful of sliced mushrooms and a few slices of tomato to sauté alongside. He shovels it all, including the browned grease, onto the large oblong platters used only for this dish and steak dinners, wraps the bacon around the sausages, nudges on a scoop of mashed potatoes, a ladle of mixed steamed (actually canned and boiled) vegetables, a stick of celery, and sometimes a couple of flowered radishes. As he lifts the finished dish onto the pickup counter he wraps the corner of his apron around his thumb and wipes the edge of the platter clean, pushes a button that rings a small chime out front, and shouts loudly into the din of the kitchen, whether there's anyone there or not, *mixee grill*!

$\mathcal{T}$HE MUFFLED SCRAPING OF

THE SNOW PLOW DOWN

on Baker Street is what he hears first. Then Coreen's deep breathing. Warmth. Shut off the alarm, quick, before she wakes up. Four forty-five, still dark, the house chilled. Dream-knot to Asia, dark and umbilical, early morning on the Pearl Delta, light the grass fire under the rice, ginger taste, garlic residue dampened. Here, on the other side of the world (through that tunnel all the way to China), in long-johns and slippers, quietly to the basement to stoke the furnace with a couple shovelfuls of coal and then wash up. Shave. He talks silently to himself (in English?) as he moves through the routine in near darkness: Who gave me this Old Spice last Christmas? One of the girls at work? Think I'll wear that rayon shirt today. Where's that pack of Players? My pen in the shirt pocket. Light brown gabardines. Start the day with less than a buck's worth of change in the right pocket. Clean hanky in the back pocket. The heavy Health Spot shoes the kids shined last night, by the kitchen door. Overcoat. Overshoes. Out the door into the morning that is still night.

Haven't plowed Victoria Street yet. Not too bad, but it's still snowing. The curling broom out of the trunk. Brush the snow off hood and windows. So quiet, he almost hates to start the Pontiac. Purr. Brr! First tracks on the street this morning, so clean. Lightly, lightly—don't lock the brakes down the hill. Good (still talking to himself), Baker Street's done. Guess I'll park out front until they get the alley plowed. Boy, the town's so quiet now. And the lights. Won't get home for a nap this afternoon. Weekend before Christmas'll be too busy for that.

The buzz of his busy day has, as every other day, kicked in through a muffled dialogue of place, person, and memory translated

3

over an intersection of anxiety, anger, and wonder at the possibility of a still new world. At least another New Year.

As he unlocks the swinging front doors of the Diamond Grill he can see the light in the kitchen at the back of the cafe and he says to himself (in Chinese?), good, Shu's already at work.

*Y*ET LANGUAGELESS. MOUTH ALWAYS
A GAUZE, WORDS LOCKED

behind tongue, stopped in and out, what's she saying, what's she want, why's she mad, this woman-silence stuck, struck, stopped— there and back, English and Chinese churning ocean, her languages caught in that loving angry rip tide of children and coercive tradition and authority. Yet.

Grampa Wah's marriage to Florence Trimble is a surprise to most of the other Chinamen in the cafes around southern Saskatchewan, but not to his wife back in China. Kwan Chungkeong comes to Canada in 1892, returns to his small village in Hoiping County in 1900, and stays just long enough to marry a girl from his village and father two daughters and a son. When he returns to Canada in 1904 he has to leave his family behind because the head tax has, in his absence, been raised to five hundred dollars (two years' Canadian wages). He realizes he'll never be able to get his family over here so, against the grain for Chinamen, he marries a white woman (Scots-Irish from Trafalgar, Ontario), the cashier in his cafe. They have three boys and four girls and he never goes back to China again.

I don't know how Grampa Wah talks her into it (maybe he doesn't) but somehow Florence lets two of her children be sent off to China as recompense in some patriarchal deal her husband has with his Chinese wife. He rationalizes to her the Confucian idea that a tree may grow as tall as it likes but its leaves will always return to the ground. Harumph, she thinks, but to no avail.

Fred and his older sister Ethel are suddenly one day in July 1916 taken to the train station in Swift Current, their train and boat tickets and identities pinned to their coats in an envelope. My grandfather had intended to send number one son but when departure day arrives Uncle Buster goes into hiding. Grampa grabs the next male in line, four-year-old Fred, and, because he is so young, nine-year-old Ethel as well, to look after him. He has the word of the conductor that the children will be delivered safely to the boat in Vancouver and from there the connections all the way to Canton have been arranged. Fred, Kwan Foo-lee, and Ethel, Kwan An-wa, spend the next eighteen years, before returning to Canada, being raised by their Chinese step-mother alongside two half-sisters and a half-brother.

Yet, in the face of this patrimonial horse-trading it is the women who turn it around for my father and Aunty Ethel. Back in Canada my grandmother, a deeply religious lady, applies years of Salvation Army morality to her heathen husband to bring her children home. But he is a gambler and, despite his wife's sadness and Christian outrage, he keeps gambling away the money that she scrapes aside for the kids' return passage.

Meanwhile, the remittance money being sent from Canada to the Chinese wife starts to dwindle when the depression hits. She feels the pinch of supporting these two half-ghosts and, besides, she reasons with my grandfather, young Foo-lee is getting dangerously attracted to the opium crowd. As a small landholder she sells some land to help buy his way back to Canada.

Aunty Ethel's situation is different. She is forced to wait while, back in Canada, Fred convinces his father to arrange a marriage for her with a Chinaman in Moose Jaw. She doesn't get back to Canada until a year later, 1935.

Yet the oceans of women migrant-tongued words in a double-bind of bossy love and wary double-talk forced to ride the waves of rebellion and obedience through a silence that shutters numb the traffic between eye and mouth and slaps across the face of family, yet these women forced to spit, out of bound-up feet and torsoed hips made-up yarns and foreign scripts unlucky colours zippered lips—

yet, to spit, when possible, in the face of the father the son the holy ticket safety-pinned to his lapel—the pileup of twisted curtains intimate ink pious pages partial pronouns translated letters shore-to-shore Pacific jetsam pretending love forgotten history braided gender half-breed loneliness naive voices degraded miscourse racist myths talking gods fact and fiction remembered faces different brothers sisters misery tucked margins whisper zero crisscross noisy mothers absent fathers high muckamuck husbands competing wives bilingual I's their unheard sighs, their yet still-floating lives.

DIRTY HEATHENS, GRANNY ERICKSON
THINKS OF THE CHINESE,

the whole bunch of them, in their filthy cafes downtown. Just because that boy dresses up and has a little money, she throws herself at him. She and those other girls, they're always horsing around, looking for fun, running off to Gull Lake for a basketball game, a bunch of little liars, messing around in those cars, I know, not getting home until late at night, all fun and no work. I know what they're doing, they can't fool me, oof dah, that Coreen, she'll ruin herself, you wait and see, she'll be back here for help soon enough. Well she can look out for herself, she's not going to get any more of my money, she can just take her medicine, now that she's living with that Chinaman, nobody'll speak to her, the little hussy.

CHINESE SAUSAGE? WHEN I'M IN
CHINATOWN I SEE

it hanging in the butcher windows in bunches, candled together with twine. My mouth waters at the sight of the dried sausages marbled with fat. I still call Chinese sausage foong cheng, that's what my Granny Wah called it. And granny cooked foong cheng nearly all the time, a real delicacy. We'd have family meals in her and Grampa's little house and there was usually a large group of people at the table, uncles and aunts and cousins. I'd watch her at the stove when she opened up the rice pot, peek at the glistening steamed sausages so red and juicy on top of the white rice. She cooked one foong cheng for each person. Everybody got served one sausage on top of their rice, and so did I, but I always had one underneath too. Granny put an extra one under my rice for me. Special.

$\mathcal{T}$o TOP IT OFF, HIS BIRTH
CERTIFICATE HAS

been destroyed in the Medicine Hat city hall fire so his parents can't prove he's Canadian. Half Chinese, speaking only Chinese and no English, arriving on a boat from Hong Kong during the paranoia of the Chinese Immigration (Exclusion) Act, my father and therefore his father can't be trusted. He's jailed in the immigration cells in Victoria, B.C., on Juan de Fuca Strait for three months while his parents try to convince immigration officials to let their son back in. They finally find some papers—his baptism records or the 1912 census—so he makes it through. His mother has her son back, his father winks, smiles, and thinks of those Confucian leaves that can be blown great distances in a strong wind.

DAD DOESN'T COOK MUCH WITH GINGER BUT WHENEVER

I accidentally bite into a piece of ginger root in the beef and greens, I make a face and put it aside. This makes him mad, not because he doesn't think ginger is bitter but because I've offended his pride in the food he prepares for us. Ginger becomes the site of an implicit racial qualification.

The other dish in which we watch out for ginger is beef and tomatoes. It floats slivered and its brassy sheen in the red sauce makes it easy to pick out.

He keeps a few inches of ginger root in the fridge freezer and slices off just a little whenever he needs it. Sparingly. Gingerly.

Though it's always used with fish because it nicely neutralizes fishy odours, ginger's delicate pungency blends deliciously in a dish of parboiled Chinese broccoli and oyster sauce. Put a couple of very thin slivers into the oyster sauce while heating it up. Spoon over the drained spears of gai lan, and serve alongside a bowl of steamed rice.

This knurled suffix of gradated foreignicity, gyna gendered and warped up tighter than a Persian rug-knot, hardly explains how ginger's almost nicer than being born—but that's just taste.

ONE OF THE FIRST TIMES
I BECOME HIM,

about fourteen years after he dies, I walk around the corner of the
garage and see a black bear in the cherry tree.

A black bear eating
in the cherry
tree.

A black bear
eating
cherries.

A black
bear.

I stand and look at that bear and sense I'm looking through my
father's face. My brow furls, squinches, partly from the sun in the
sky behind the trees. This frown isn't at the bear so much as at the
whole world. I'm looking into the black bear's eyes through my
father's. This isn't unpleasant, just sort of glowering, quizzical,
dark, storm, cloud.

I feel decanting through my body his ocean (I think I can even
smell it), all he could ever comprehend in a single view; that this is,
in me, part of some same helical sentence we both occupy, the asyn-
chronous grains of sand along a double-helix dream time track, the
déjà vu of body, skin and fur and eyes, a brief intersection of animal
coordinates.

Synapse and syntax: the bear returns to eating the cherries.

_T_HEY WOULDN'T SPEAK TO ME
UNTIL AFTER YOU

were born, my mother explains when I ask her how people in Swift Current reacted to her marrying a Chinaman.

More than a year they wouldn't speak to me. They were really mad you know, because they were bigots, they were racists. Scandinavians are generally fairly racist, at least they were in those days. Not all of them, but a lot of them are. They see themselves as a pure race, something like the Germans, Aryan.

And of course my brother-in-law made things worse because he really shot his mouth off, he really antagonized my father and mother against your father. That wasn't any help. He refused to let me see my sister, you know, he wouldn't let me in their house. He said I disgraced the whole family, all that stuff.

I was hurt, but I loved your dad and that was it. So I made my choices and I wasn't sorry, I never felt bad about that.

Eventually, after you were born, my parents asked me to come around. They wanted to see you.

It was more my mother's problem, though. Dad eventually accepted your father and really liked him after he got to know him. But my mom always seemed to feel like I had made a mistake. She always felt like she'd been hard done by. Really, she was mad for the rest of her life. None of her daughters married who she wanted. She always regretted leaving Sweden. She was forever complaining to Dad. He could have taken a job in Göteborg. Now here they were stuck on this godforsaken prairie with little money and few friends and him building grain elevators out there miles from nowhere, and drinking beer, too. So that really put her in a huff when I ran off and married a Chinese.

I think, eventually, in the end, she liked your dad. He was a good father, because your dad didn't drink or anything you know, he was a good provider.

I didn't lose too many friends when I married your dad. You sure learn who your friends are when you marry outside your own race. My best friend, the one I sometimes visit up in Calgary, when she got married her husband wouldn't allow her to invite us to the wedding and that hurt both her and me very badly. And then I lost touch with her for awhile. Wasted years, you know, people are so stupid, they waste their lives. Like my sister said, the years we've wasted, of not knowing each other, of our families not knowing each other, just over the fact your dad was Chinese, even only part Chinese.

But there was a lot of racism in those days, you know. It isn't like it is now, a completely accepted thing at all. No one says anything now about anyone marrying a Chinese or a Japanese or whatever they marry.

But all that's in the past. I've forgotten a lot of things. Your dad, he just shrugged it off, though I know it hurt him. I didn't think of him as Chinese or anything. I just loved him. You should have asked me before. I could have told you. Why do you want to write about this anyway? That's all done with.

5:30 A.M. BY THE TIME
HE WALKS INTO

the kitchen. Shu's already got things going at the stove.

Shu grunts, Hey, how'r you?

Pretty good. And, because it's Friday December 21 and the cafe will be very busy and because Christmas is his favourite time of the year, he does feel pretty good today. Anything yet?

No, I thought they might phone last night. Shu leans on the cutting board with one hand and the permanent cigarette stuck to his lips. I know the boat docked o.k. but Joe Chow hasn't called me. I hope those immigration guys don't make a problem.

He snorts with scorn. Those dog ghosts. Don't worry, they just get high-muckamuck for awhile, it goes with the uniform. It'll work out, you'll see. He'll probably wire you today.

Shu's been waiting most of the week for word of his wife and teen-age son. For nearly two years now he has tried to arrange for them to leave China and join him in Canada. Shu hasn't seen them for thirteen years, and now they're almost here. Shu's bought a house in Nelson and they're supposed to come up on the train from Vancouver as soon as they clear immigration. Joe Chow, the Chinese lawyer, has looked after all the paper work and talked to all the government people. Everything's set and Shu doesn't want it to go wrong.

He grabs the clean cotton coffee-filter sacks and an arm-load of saucers and kicks the kitchen door to the dining room. The place looks warm and tidy in the soft glow from the big Wurlitzer which is always left on. He flicks on the overheads and moves straight to the coffee urn up by the front counter.

Yes sir, this is gonna be a good weekend, even if it does snow a lot.

*W*HENEVER I OPEN UP FOR HIM (SO HE

can sleep in) early morning's dark eternal neon Wurlitzer shadowing the empty booths detonates with kicking the kitchen door a starting-pistol crack all through the cafe I know I'm both only me and all of me at full stride up the aisle with clean cotton coffee-filter sacks and an arm-load of saucers echoed ache of brass plate in my leg eternal, ready Freddy, open up with a good swift toe to the wooden slab that swings between the Occident and Orient to break the hush of the whole cafe before first light the rolling gait with which I ride this silence that is a hyphen and the hyphen is the door.

I GUESS HE'S PEEVED ENOUGH AT ALL THE

shit he's going through back in Canada, the immigration jail, this so-called family, father mother brothers sisters most of whom he can hardly remember and some he's never met, his older sister left behind in China, pretty much languageless except for the cooks in the cafe, this cold, dry prairie after lush and humid Cantonese landscape, no friends, strange music, white farmers in coveralls and white bankers in business suits—screw that.

As soon as he's picked up enough English to get by, it takes him just a few more months after getting to Swift Current to high-tail it to the Lakehead at Port Arthur. He knows a Chinaman can always find his way around the country by knocking on the kitchen doors of Chinese restaurants. He has his eye on sneaking into the States and getting a job as a cook on a freighter. This Great Lakes caper doesn't last long though because he jumps ship in Chicago (another distant island in my blood) and is picked up right away for illegal entry. After a few weeks in jail the immigration people have him figured out and soon he's back in Swift Current working in the Elite on Central Avenue, not the Regal, which is the one his father owns around the corner, across from the railway station.

He seems to have buckled down after this because then he marries my mom, they have their first two boys, and after the war move out to Trail, B.C.

So that's what he says or thinks, doesn't he? Buckle down, have a family of your very own, slip memory under each day's work, under your brown skin, under the buckle, the belt. Tuck away the questions. Just put your nose to the grind. Up that hill and fetch that pail of spitting image. Do what the father's fathers tell you; their words are your commands. First get a job get married get a house get a car (isn't that right?)—then you can breathe easy. Take charge of your life, but if you take after him who do I take after? Let me remember what history repeats. History repeats. Imitate everything but copy nothing. Politics is in your pocket. That piggy bank will someday be a Cadillac. The mathematics of the family is a music whose notes are not heard. Pick up the beat when the drummer stops. He's done all of this so you won't step into his shoes. Dismantle the mantle. Devolve the valve. Chip into the blood bank. Kill the will. Inherit the hostage. Suss the ancest. When you grow up.

But until then. Get cracking!

*B*Y THE TIME HE GETS OVER
FEELING SPOOKED

he's twenty-three years old and working in a small cafe in a small town sixty miles north of Swift Current. His father arranges a live-in job for him at the Elite Cafe in Cabri with a couple of gambling acquaintances named Shorty and Slim. He goes to school in his spare time to learn English. Everyone, including his father, mother, brothers, sisters, are, at first, strangers and the only people he can talk to are the Chinese, his father and the cooks in the cafe. But he picks up enough English and cafe-business smarts to move back to Swift Current within a year and by 1936 he's wearing a suit and tie and taking in every Swift Current Indians home game he can. He loves hockey but never learns to skate.

𝓗IS MOTHER'S FAMILY ARE STERN AND
RELIGIOUS SCOTS/IRISH

railroad people from Ontario. His in-laws, when he marries Coreen Erickson in 1938, are post-WWI economic refugees from Sweden. While he and Ethel have been in China, their brothers and sisters have negotiated particular identities for themselves through the familiarity of a white European small prairie town commonality (albeit colonial democracy). Though he arrives back to everyone struggling through the thirties, they all have their place. They're part of the reputed latest Pleistocene migration staged to the middle of Canada. And they are, then, him and then his and her, and then me and so on, given the impediment, authority and, above all, the possibility of place. He thinks, after he and Ethel's intimidation as half-ghosts in China, that this Petri dish of hope and plenty is a great opportunity through which (and with which) he and his kind can go on, away from, hopefully, the fragmented diaspora, but always with some tag of chance that will continually fire a brand-spanking new trajectory into what has been, after all, an unrelentingly foreign world. Hybridize or disappear; family *in* place.

THOSE DOORS TAKE QUITE A BEATING. BRASS

sheet nailed across the bottom. *Whap!* What a way to announce your presence. You kind of explode, going through one door onto the customers, through the other onto the cooks. It's so nifty when I discover how they work: you're supposed to go through only on the right-hand side and that's how you don't get hit not looking when someone steamrollers through the other door at full clip with a load of dirty dishes or food spread out along their hands and arms. *Boom!* You'd think the glass portholes'd fall out of the doors, but they're built to take it. Inch-and-a-half varnished fir plywood with big spring hinges. When I first start working in the cafe I love to wallop that brass as hard as I can. But my dad warns me early to not make such a noise because that disturbs the customers, so I come up with a way of placing my heel close to the bottom and then rocking the foot forward to squeeze the door open in a silent rush of air as I come through on the fly. But when we get real busy, like at lunchtime, all the waiters and waitresses, including my dad, will let loose in the shape and cacophony of busy-ness, the kicker of desire hidden in the isochronous torso, a necessary dance, a vital percussion, a critical persuasion, a playful permission fast and loud, *WhapBamBoom!*—feels so good.

𝒯HESE STRAITS AND ISLANDS

OF THE BLOOD CAN

be recognized as those very shores and lands we encounter in our earthly migrations. Places become buttons of feeling and colour. *Pudeur*, a sudden heat or blush, ferments the recognitions. Whole worlds genetically traced. I know, for example, the coagulation of Victoria on Hong Kong Island and Victoria on Vancouver Island have become, in my inheritance, planetary junctures of deep emotion. Both British Victorias, these new-world cities must have seemed to my ancestors two ends of the same rope. But many of the Chinamen, when they got to Canadian Victoria, were locked up in the Detention Hospital, a pigpen of iron screens and doors used for interrogation and the collection of head taxes. My father was held there. He told me that earlier Gold Mountain men had inked or scratched poems on the walls that expressed their sorrow and anguish at being held there.

Detained on this island
at the gates of Gold Mountain
brings to my throat a hundred feelings.
. . .
My heart is filled with a sadness
and anger I don't understand.
. . .
Day after day
how can I vent my hatred
but through these lines?

. . .

The fog horns in the distance
only deepen my sadness.

Biology recapitulates geography; place becomes an island in the
blood.

*P*ONG SHOWS UP AT ANY TIME IN THE MORNING,

whenever he feels like it. He's the silent partner in the business and doesn't draw a wage; just lets his money work for him. He's smoking a cigarette, sipping a cup of coffee, and lounging on a Coke crate when Fred comes into the kitchen. They don't say anything to each other. Pong's in the middle of yapping about his wife. She never gave him any children and now she's too old. Why bring her over? he shrugs at Fred, who just keeps moving. Shu doesn't say anything either, he's busy buttering toast, cooking.

You know, she got to Hong Kong and now she lives the good life, at her sister's. She wants more money every month. But I told her no, I'm going to come to Hong Kong and see her soon, so I need the money for the trip.

Pong's been talking about this trip for over a year now. No one doubts he'll go but they know he won't bring his wife to Canada. Why bother? She'd just get in the way of his gambling, and Pong is one of the most notorious gamblers in western Canada. He goes to Calgary and Vancouver all the time. Sometimes he comes back spiffy, new suit, gold rings, and all smiles. Other times he's lost everything, grouchy until he starts winning again.

Pong ends up yapping mostly to the swinging glass portals of the kitchen doors; the three working partners don't have a lot of time for talk during one of the busiest weekends of the year.

FAMOUS CHINESE RESTAURANT
IS THE NAME OF A

small, strip-mall Chinese cafe a friend of mine eats at once in awhile. We laugh at the innocent pretentiousness of the name, Famous.

But then I think of the pride with which my father names the Diamond Grill. For him, the name is neither innocent nor pretentious. The Diamond, he proudly regales the banquet at the grand opening, is the most modern, up-to-date restaurant in the interior of B.C. The angled design of the booths matches the angles of a diamond and the diamond itself stands for good luck. We hope this new restaurant will bring good luck for all our families and for this town. Eat! Drink! Have a good time!

Almost everything in Chinese stands for good luck, it seems. You're not supposed to use words that might bring bad luck. Aunty Ethel is very upset when we choose a white casket for my father's funeral. She says, that no good! White mean death, bad luck!

So I understand something of the dynamics of naming and desire when I think of the names of some Chinese cafes in my family's history. The big one, of course, is the Elite, which we, with no disrespect for the Queen's English, always pronounce the eee-light. In fact, everyone in town pronounces it that way. My dad works in an Elite in Swift Current and that's what he names his cafe in Trail when we move out to B.C. Elite is a fairly common Chinese cafe name in the early fifties, but not any more. I see one still on Edmonton Trail in Calgary and I know of one in Revelstoke. I like the resonant undertone in the word *élite*: the privilege to choose. In the face of being denied the right to vote up until 1949, I smile a little at the recognition by the Chinese that choice is, indeed, a privilege.

Other names also play on the margins of fantasy and longing.

Grampa Wah owns the Regal in Swift Current and just around the corner are the Venice and the Paris. Just as Chiang escapes to Taiwan my father gets into the New Star in Nelson.

During the fifties and sixties, coincidental with the rise of Canadian nationalism, we find small-town cafes with names like the Canadian, Canada Chinese Take-Out, and, in respect of Hockey Night in Canada, the All Star. Along the border: American-Canadian Cafe and the Ambassador.

One could read more recent trends such as Bamboo Terrace, Heaven's Gate, Pearl Seafood Restaurant, and the Mandarin as indicative of both the recognized exoticization in orientalism as well as, possibly, a slight turn, a deference, pride and longing for the homeland.

Perhaps we might regard more concretely what resonates for us when we walk into places like White Dove Cafe and Hotel in Mossbank Saskatchewan or the even-now famous Disappearing Moon Cafe, 50 East Pender Street, Vancouver, B.C.

ONCE IN THE NEW WORLD,
THE IMMIGRANT CAN

develop images of place that become cankers of irritation. Some mass or weight of space, arena, feels heavy with the debt of the new. Bitter Gold Mountain. Bitter Saskatchewan.

No history of Cabri would be complete without a few lines about the Chinese who operated some of the businesses, and lived in Cabri. They were no different from other people who came to make their homes and build a new life. These quiet industrious little men had no wives or families, most of their earnings went back home to the homeland to support families they'd left behind.

Most of those who came to Cabri went into the restaurant business, they soon became well known to a great many people and made many friends.

One of the first to come was Woo Sing in 1913, who was a tailor by trade. He is reported to have done some laundry business at one time. Over many of the years he spent here his main activity was tailoring, with dry cleaning as a sideline. He left here in 1969.

Joe Yee opened a restaurant in 1914, known as Quick Lunch, and continued for nearly 40 years. His cook over most of those years was a small man with a big smile known as Snow Ball. The two of them were a very popular team, they carried on until 1952 when the business was sold to At and Mollie Harris.

Quan Hall opened a restaurant in 1918, in a building on Main Street about where the present home of Clifford Fahselt now stands. He ran this place for a number of years, it was closed in the mid 1930's and was torn down not too long after it was vacated. Quan was a congenial fellow, especially fond of small children, which he greeted with much talk and many treats.

Shorty opened the Elite Cafe in 1921, approximately where the present entrance of the Co-op Store is now. His cook and helper for many years was known as Slim.

These two were a rather solemn pair, although Shorty had a fairly short fuse when riled. He had an abacus which he kept in reach, did most of his calculation on it, as much as people today use a calculator. The two ran a good restaurant and were in business until about 1954-55.

Joe Yee and Snow Ball, with help from Woo Sing, were responsible for introducing the old oriental gambling game Mah Jhong to the young fellows in Cabri. The game wasn't easy to play, the first sets to appear here were marked only in Chinese. Later on sets marked with both English and Chinese arrived, making it much easier to play the game, but it is seldom played here any more.

No Chinese women were allowed to enter the country until recently, A certain number of males could come in and for the Chinese living in Cabri it was possible to have a son, grandson or nephew brought into the country. They were educated in the local school and trained in business by their sponsor. These boys in turn went into business on their own.

Over the years a great many took their schooling here. Harry Wong stayed for quite a few years as well as Shorty and Slim. Later on Harry acquired a farm in the Roseray District. After some time, he sold the farm and moved to Lethbridge where he operated a convenience store for many years.

Charlie Quan purchased Molly's Inn and operated it from 1956-1969.

In 1970, Peter, Susy Wong and family continued the restaurant business and are still here in 1984 operating the Silver Cafe.

(from *Through the Years: History of Cabri and District,* Cabri History Book Committee, 1984)

*a*s soon as the cafe
opens at quarter

to six, half a dozen regulars stumble in and stake out their spots, mostly up at the counter. They just want coffee and gossip, the weather and roads, hockey games this weekend, Smokies, Flyers, Dynamiters, Maple Leafs, some bets, some laughs. Jeez, that Grant Warwick's a crazy sonofabitch. Hey Freddy, grab me a pack of Craven A will you?

A few have just come off graveyard at the CPR and others are on their way to work. The highways engineer leaves his pickup running while he and his gofer grab a coffee. It's still dark out and snowing but there are headlights moving on Baker Street. A cab driver comes in for a coffee-to-go. No one on cash yet so some of them just leave their dime at the till.

He asks Sandy the contractor about his riff with the building inspector. He knows Sandy is riled up and will welcome the chance to spout off to the guys about those godamn paper pushers at city hall. He listens to the banter and then cracks some joke about how Sandy couldn't be getting enough tail. He says *tail* with an emphatic grimace as if he were mouthing a foreign word. They all laugh it up and Sandy just mumbles, throws a dime on the counter, and quips back at him about how a Chinaman who can't take out an unguarded rock in the centre of the circle probably couldn't find a hole. He laughs with them. They're his customers, he wants them to come back.

After they leave, empty their ashtrays onto a saucer and wipe the counter. Make way for more coffee and breakfasts. Stack a butter! Ham and scrambled! Bowl a mush! That first hour before Donna comes on at seven is a mild rush, no time, just him and the cook, get the backup urn of coffee ready, hasn't eaten yet, a quick sip of coffee on the run, so blast and run the morning into the day, day after day until he dies, until the rampaged blood is seedless, until the leaning heart is sacked.

*T*HE SILENT ANGER SIMMERS,

OVER SOME FAILED EXPECTATION,

words useless because either what's done is done or the counter logic too grinding to overcome. But anger at the silence itself, at the languagelessness, unable to speak the English they natter at him when he steps off the boat, gets back home: Welcome back, this is your mother, these are your brothers and sisters!—after seventeen years of not so much being away as being the other, the foreign son, part-ghost, other side of the world, digging straight through the centre, growing up China-Chinese and through the same mouthless anger arriving there and back again both times stopped stunned and caught in this double-bind of other information, Chinese-Canadian, Chinese-white, hyphenated tongue-tied vacant humming shoulder-deep, such a wooden little boy in his black wool turtle-neck, horizons signed alone, eyes all dark alone and cold and come no nearer—that anger at not having language itself, never mind the words—that much anger, at the empty, emptied, voice except behind his eyes the absence clouded shuttled ocean washed up along his brow just another line of chippy foam. Wave. Whoosh.

I TELL HIM IF HE GETS HER A

Mixmaster for Christmas we'll be able to make milkshakes at home just like at the cafe.

The milkshake mixer we have at the Diamond is a deluxe Hamilton Beach, pastel green, with five beaters. Very modern. When the milkshake can is lifted up to the beater it fits snugly into two metal snaps, one of which is a switch. Automatic. Easy to clean, too. Fill a milkshake can with hot water, slip it up to a beater, let it run for a few seconds, and then dry off the beater with a cloth.

The milkshake cans are heavy duty stainless and each one can hold enough to make two shakes. The normal shake takes a little less than half a can of milk, a scoop of vanilla, and two squirts of flavouring.

For my friends I make extra thick shakes by using up to three scoops of ice cream. Mike Horswill comes in and asks for an extra thick shake, at least four scoops of ice cream. Chocolate I think. Dairy Queen has just moved into town and Mike's enthusiastic about their ultra-thick milkshakes. He says they're so thick you can hold them upside down and they won't spill. He'll happily pay twice the Diamond's price of twenty cents if I make him a four-scoop shake. I do. I deliver an almost solid mass of whipped ice cream to his booth; he can hardly get his straw into it. He looks around at all the kids at the table kind of showing off this extra-special shake. Tom Carney says hey Mike I bet you can't hold that shake upside down! Horsewill bets him a chocolate Coke and a doughnut and then turns his shake upside down. Plop! It's a mess on the table. We all have a good laugh and Mike turns a little red. The Dairy Queen serves their shakes in cardboard containers. The Diamond uses real milkshake glasses. That must be the difference.

*A*T THE FRONT OF THE DIAMOND GRILL ARE

two horseshoe-shaped counters (the horseshoe design adds to the luck; I can tell, by the big smile Grampa always has on his face when he slaps his lottery book down on those counters). Surrounding each counter are ten chrome and Naugahyde stools that spin freely. A little ledge under the counter can hold gloves and purses and someone always comes running back in after lunch and peeks under the counter for something they've left behind. Charlie Boyd's dad left his spud under there, a small potato that he carries in his pocket to ward off warts.

Each counter has three chrome fence-units with special slots for the menus; here's where we set out the napkin dispenser, salt and pepper, and a sugar jar with a shiny chrome screw-on pouring lid. With the two juke boxes on each counter, there's quite a bit of chrome to keep polished on those counters. Behind and under the counters we keep the sauces (HP, steak sauce, Tabasco, ketchup, and, in the mornings, the pancake syrup dispensers which also have screw-on chrome pouring lids), cutlery trays, and extra saucers, ashtrays, and other odds and ends. A singular omnipotence and authority is available when serving from within the centre of these corrals.

These two counters have been designed for maximum use of a small space and are laid out to form one continuous unit running past the soda fountain and up to the till. The only door in this Arborite feedlot is really a gate between the first counter seat and the glass display case of the till and can only be opened by those of us who know how to operate its very modern latch, hidden so you have to finger it from the bottom. This cafe is the newest and most modern establishment in Nelson (before the new Greyhound depot) and, of all of its doors, I enjoy this gate with the secret latch, this early instance of the power that comes from camouflage and secrecy.

*S*HE COMPLAINED, MY MOTHER
SAYS OF GRANNY ERICKSON,

that she had to stand there on the street outside the beer parlour and, because she wasn't allowed in unescorted, tried to get one of the men to get him out for her. That's when she was really mad at him. Daggers in her eyes.

Usually, at home, she just said what's the matter with you, you crazy old man. You're not going downtown today. And don't you chew that snoose in my house. What a dirty old man you are.

And Grampa'd rise to the bait and blurt something out in Swedish and then sulk and stew around the house like a scolded pup. He didn't drink that often. At house parties he might have a couple more beer than he could handle and then he'd loosen up and call her a silly old cow, maybe try to pinch her on the tit. She just scowled back at him.

Then she'd say Oof Dah, that man, he drinks too much! Oof Dah!

*T*HE RACE TRACK? SWEDISH, CHINESE,
SCOTTISH, IRISH, CANADIAN.

You bet. But somewhere in that stable the purebreds dissolve into paints. The starting gate opens as my father's face implanted on my scowly brow, body rigid. Parts folding into body after body. His father Lucky Jim on the porch singing old Chinese nursery rhymes, tears but a gold-toothed smile always. My mother a smiler too, then her father sour, her mother more sour yet. Temper. The teacher telling us who we get to be, to write down what our fathers are. Race, race, race. English, German, Doukhobor, Italian. But not Canadian, there's a difference between a race and a country. No matter what, you're what your father is, was, forever. After school. Chink, Limy, Kraut, Wop, Spik. The whole town. Better than the Baker Street nickel millionaires my dad calls them. Race makes you different, nationality makes you the same. Sameness is purity. Not the same anything when you're half Swede, quarter Chinese, and quarter Ontario Wasp. The Salvation Army my granny marches with, into the parade of other grannies, uncles, aunts, cousins, half quarter full and distant, all waiting for Saskatchewan to appear for them. Stuttered inventive, invective process. The domain of this track is an ordered fiction, a serious intervention. Until we now know the only fiction here has to be the reader. You know, relative.

them break an egg into the coffee grounds, turn taps, fill cream jugs, body picks up speed. A little spark to the step starts. Unlock the front door and switch on the neon sign. At Christmas, there're those lights and decorations to turn on. Ring through the cash register until the receipt printout prints o.k. Set out the stack of *Nelson Daily News* up front next to the till.

This is work. Rhythm. Don't love it but count on it, get into it. Some kind of dance; patterned yet yielding at the edges, room for subtle improv. Things touch and snap and flip and the shoulders and arms feel loose and precise, measured.

Like the spring my Uncle Buster comes out from Swift Current and works at the Diamond for a few months. Buster's hands are so big he can span and pick up a dinner plate like a basketball. He and my dad work in sync, animate a plate or a fork on the go, make the day hum.

Buster's the number one son and even though he hid out the day he was to be sent to China and my father was sent as his replacement, they get along just fine. Bus is a great kidder and quite laid back, as they say. His voice is husky and must be the reason for his nickname.

But what's so striking about Buster are his hands. They're not only large but in tune. So sensitive to surface that utensils, plates, cups, glasses, quarters, dimes, and nickels juggle through the air in perfect arcs of utility, always landing with precision. He has touch, he's a pro, and he's taught me how to make a quarter walk on the countertop. Spin.

OLD MAN HANSEN COMES IN AT TEN TO

six, when things aren't even ready yet. He's always the first. He takes a paper and puts a dime on the stack, and then shuffles down to booth number three, hangs up his hat and overcoat, and sits facing the front, silent and stonefaced. Hansen is in his eighties, always wears a dark suit, rooms alone down at the Arlington, depends on the Diamond for breakfast and some suppers. The cafe even opens by six on Christmas and New Years mornings so Hansen will be able to get breakfast. Wordlessly, Fred brings Hansen his coffee and a jug of syrup on the way to the kitchen to order. Stack a hot! Side a sausage!

Shu, the cook, doesn't even look up. He's ready. He echoes stack a hot! and his hands sweep up the bowl of batter and ladle three perfect pancakes already on the grill. He's been waiting for that first order shouted into the kitchen air. That's the switch, the buzz. Now the day has measure.

𝒥'M FAIRLY BLOND IN GRADE
FOUR AND STILL

she calls me a Chink. Out loud in the schoolyard at Central School, and with her eyes too, real daggers, a painful spike. Never mind the problems my father has from both the Chinese (he's a half-breed, he's really a white man, he's married to a white woman) and the Wasps (he looks Chinese, he can talk Chinese, and he runs the cafe, right?)

But what about me? I don't look Chinese. I'm pretty white. I have a lot of good friends, play hockey and trumpet. But the first girl I get serious about is from one of the town's high muckamuck families; her father's a local lumber baron. They put up with me for a little while but when things get hot she's sent away to Spokane to live with her older sister because her father doesn't want his daughter marrying a Chinaman. He tells me that one night when he comes home late and catches us parked, necking in the alley behind their big house. He says I've got nothing against you or your family but I don't want my daughter marrying a Chinaman. It just can't work. What a bastard. He says to me Look I know your father's a respected business man downtown but you've got sneaky eyes and I don't want you seeing my daughter any more so don't let me catch you around here again and no more phone calls either. Well fuck! I can't even speak Chinese my eyes don't slant and aren't black my hair's light brown and I'm not going to work in a restaurant all my life but I'm going to go to university and I'm going to be as great a fucking white success as you asshole and my name's still going to be Wah and I'll love garlic and rice for the rest of my life.

My brother does manage to marry her sister, though.

STAINLESS STEEL ALL ALONG THE

SODA FOUNTAIN, SILVER

bright, row of lids for the syrups. The strawberry one is the hardest to keep clean, real strawberries. Hard red jewels congeal on the shiny chrome each day. Forever mopping up with clean white cloths, running water, slooshing the glasses in suds over a brush built into the sink. All the glasses get washed up front, only the dishes go to the kitchen. In 1951 the Diamond's got the most modern soda fountain in town. More flavours than anyone. Besides lemon Cokes we serve both cherry and chocolate Cokes, though the lemon Cokes are the most popular; just a wedge of fresh lemon floating there with the ice cubes on top of the bubbles. A friend tells me that down at the Standard they slice the lemon instead of wedge it and he prefers ours because it's easier to squeeze the lemon.

The marshmallow is the stickiest. Comes solidified in large cans from Malkins. We have to put the can in some hot water to make it flow, sometimes even cut it with a bit of hot water just to ladle it out. Besides the marshmallow, the other things ladled are cherries, strawberries, and pineapple. Things like chocolate, orange, raspberry, and Coke come as syrups and can be dispensed plunger-style into or onto whatever concoction. Carbonated water is pumped up to the fountain from the basement and fizzes out of futuristic-looking nozzles with big hand-hold levers on top. We mix ginger ale from syrup and carbonated water. Post-war modernity effervescent, sleek and gleaming like the two-door light blue Pontiac fast-back my dad buys, our first brand new car.

The ice cream (chocolate, strawberry, or vanilla) is in cardboard tubs in a refrigerated unit under six well-hinged thunky stainless lids. Each lid has a little knob tipped with rubber so you can fling the lid open, grab a scooper with a spring-loaded thumb trigger from the built-in porcelain water container, reach down into the tub almost up to your shoulder and ream out a scoop trying not to get any on your knuckles. Each lid has a good rubber seal so when you flip it closed during the rush there's the muffled thunk syncopated to the dance of plates and ringing till and heel and toe on floor and door. Deep apple pie á la mode, banana split, neapolitan, chocolate-marshmallow sundae, and one year I concoct the Grey Cup Special: three scoops, maple-walnut, chocolate and pineapple syrup ringed with bananas and strawberries topped with coconut, maraschino cherry, and whipped cream, the works for thirty-nine cents.

But when business is slow, as the soda jerk I have to wipe all that stainless to a dazzle and wash, rinse, and dry the glasses.

That soda fountain has to sparkle, Freddy, my dad warns. It's your job to keep it neat, clean, and ready—real pizzaz, ya understand?

And I do. The soda fountain becomes my territory. If a waitress needs a milkshake a sundae a Coke or whatever, she has to order it from me. When my friends come in after school I impress them by serving up larger-than-normal scoops of ice cream, thicker shakes, more sauce, and fancier flourishes of whipped cream. I'm the only one, except my dad, who knows how to put a scoop of ice cream in a soda so that it doesn't fizz over.

So I say to my dad, sure, I can do that. I can make this the smoothest, shiniest, snazziest soda fountain in town. You'll see!

$\mathcal{B}$UT I'M HALF SWEDISH. MY
MOTHER WAS BORN

Karin Marie Erickson in Sala, Sweden, a little west of Uppsala, historical royal seat of the Vikings. In 1922, at the age of six, she and a brother and sister emigrated with their parents to Swift Current. They lived on a farm for a year before moving into town where her father got work as a carpenter. He spent most of his life on the prairies nailing up grain elevators.

The family knew a few Swedes in the Swift Current area, like the Ahlstroms who farmed out at Waldec, and quite a few had moved into southern Saskatchewan from Minnesota after the war. My mother's parents didn't speak Swedish at home so the kids would learn English quickly. She says everyone was from somewhere else in the world and little attention was paid to race or ethnicity. Difference was common.

Connie worked in Cooper's Department Store part-time and stayed on there full-time after high school. One dollar a day, 8:30 in the morning until ten at night. She saved enough to buy a winter coat, a good one, four dollars and fifty cents, the one she's wearing in the photo as she looks into the baby buggy.

She played on a women's basketball team and met my dad at a basketball game in Gull Lake in September of 1937. They played on an outdoor court since there were no gyms in the schools in those days. The times were tough but she says my dad always had some money in his pocket. Years later he advised me to get into the food business. He said you'll never get rich but everybody has to eat so you'll always make enough to get by.

She married my dad a year later and was shunned by her family for marrying a Chinaman. At least until I was born; my blond hair

and blue eyes enough to ease her parents' anxiety about the colour of
their grandson's skin.

MY SISTER SAYS TOMATO BEEF IS ENOUGH TO

make her go back to eating meat. This is a really good gingery winter dish, particularly as a leftover when you get home late from playing hockey and it's still warm on top of the stove.

Use nine to ten small tomatoes or a forty-eight ounce can, stewed or whole. Stir-fry strips of beef with about a thumb of sliced ginger, one or two cloves of crushed garlic, a chopped onion, and a ladle full of soy sauce. Add tomatoes, one tsp. sugar, a little salt, and simmer to boil down a bit to stew-like consistency. Add some diced celery about ten minutes before serving. Spoon over top of rice and pick out pungent chunks of ginger and hide under bowl.

*T*AKEOUT AT THE DIAMOND IS
USUALLY JUST SANDWICHES.

Nothing like the styrofoam fortune cookie Chinese takeout cuisine available throughout most cities in North America today. The Chinese section of the menu is actually quite small. Just a dozen or so items: chicken or pork chow mein, sweet and sour spareribs, noodle soup, beef and broccoli, chicki fly lice as the cooks in the kitchen humorously respond, the good old standby, egg foo yung, and so forth. You might get an order for some Chinese food late at night from the gamblers upstairs, two doors away, at the Percolator Club or maybe someone working late at an office, but the Chinese takeout in the Diamond is nothing like the popular gluey Authentic Cantonese, Szechuan and Hunan Takeout and Delivery that has become the Friday-night fare of families nowadays.

The only delivery we have is Dad who the police sometimes call after a busy Saturday night to bring some hot meals down to what he humorously calls the Gow-ol (because of the engraved sign of Gaol over the door).

One of the biggest takeout orders we ever have, and one of the most unusual, since the Doukhobors are vegetarian, is when a whole bunch of Sons of Freedom are arrested. Buckets of salad are sent up to the jail and Dad keeps running back for more salad oil (he says he saw one guy literally drink it from the bottle). But sometimes he stays up at the temporary outdoor compound where the arrested Doukhobors are kept and he'll eat with them. There's a picture of him sitting at a table with a group of kerchiefed women—bottles of ketchup, plates of vegetables, rice, and potatoes, loaves of Toast-master 4x bread. He thinks they're pretty strange but he gets along with them and some of the ones who've got out of jail on bail come into the cafe to eat and see him. They have Shu's daily vegetable soup and thicken it with copious amounts of ketchup.

The other big takeout order we get is during the summer when the forest service phones in a big order for the firefighters; frequently it will be something like two hundred bag lunches to be picked up in two hours. Shu sets up the assembly line in the kitchen and anyone who can be spared from the front is expected to help wrap and stuff sandwiches in the bags with oranges, apples, matrimonial cake, and sliced carrots and celery.

When Mrs. Davis, one of our regulars who works at Eaton's, breaks her leg, Dad fixes up her favourite sausages and gravy over mashed potatoes with sauerkraut on the side and takes it up to her a few times during her convalescence.

But the best takeout is to our house. We get as much of Seto's leftover pastry and pie as we want and frequently Dad arrives home with the remains of some real Chinese food cooked by Shu—ox tail soup, deep fried cod, chicken with pineapple and lichee—things we don't always taste willingly but forever after crave.

BUT POOR MOM. SHE KNOWS
THE GIRLS DON'T

like garlic breath on her boys so she always reminds us to eat some parsley after dinner before we go out on a date. Well Dad has a bird over that. What's the matter with us. He doesn't worry about his breath. Garlic's good enough for him. What makes us think we're so much better than he is. He tells Mom she's crazy for getting us to chew parsley.

Actually that same girl who isn't allowed to bear my children does complain once about my garlic breath. I tell her she's nuts, I can't smell a thing and all she has to do is eat some garlic each night for supper and everything'll be cool.

Tonight I cook some lai foon with vegetables in a black bean and garlic sauce. I turn the fan on over the stove to take the smell out— just in case someone drops by.

SHE CRIES FROM ANGER. THAT'S
WHAT SHE TELLS

me. Her tears are from anger.

I didn't know that (strangle of fire within). Really. I thought when she cried (eyes shut tight in a dog-star head) it was because she was disappointed (wrath-rush blood in a heart-hot chest), usually in me (count to ten).

Or maybe just pent-up inside (cacophonous noise) at the dark outside (suckled at the wolf's lip). A little heavy weather (rain on ripe corn), distant thunder passing.

But not that, that . . . (wind in the trees).

But now I know she's angry when she cries, what can I do or say?

After all, the anger's hers. I can't feel it for her.

She says to me one night, Stop! You don't have to say anything more than what you just said.

*O*N MY SWEDISH SIDE
I FEEL MORE GLOOM

than anger. Oof dah my grandmother would say. And poor old Grampa Erickson always seemed to be caught under her dark cloud at home.

In contrast, my mother has always shown quite a good humour and I hope I got away with a bit of it. My wife says she married me for my smile. But lately she observes to me my doom and gloom, my fretting, furrowed brow, my blond old-world becoming habit grouchiness, my Scandinavian Lutheran chronicle looms Leif Eriksson's wintered worrying treaded L'Anse Aux Meadow Vinland map Atlantic treed horizon Europe treeless after all.

$\mathcal{I}$'M A CHINTZY TIPPER IN
RESTAURANTS BECAUSE I'M

quite critical of the service and the problem usually starts right off the top when I have to ask the waiter or waitress for a glass of water. Don't they know any better?

Early in my training at the Diamond Grill my dad scolds me for going to a table without water. He says you always start with a glass of water. That's the very first thing you do. You show up at the table with menus and water. The water is like a welcome. The customer sees you care about them, that you're ready to get them some food. And you keep that water glass filled the whole time they're eating. That keeps you going back to their table and that's good because they might want something else and they won't have to try to get your attention. That's service. That's what you get paid for and that's how you earn tips.

But don't forget, the glasses have to be clean. Serve a glass of water with lipstick on the rim and you're in trouble. A customer sees that and they might just walk right out. So always check the glasses when you're filling them.

Water's the most important thing in a restaurant. It should be cold and clear, particularly on hot days. It's the only thing that's free but it's the key to running a good cafe. Don't you forget it.

The Way We Serve Milk
at the Diamond

has been modernized by Palm Dairies. Until recently, when a customer ordered milk, white or chocolate, we'd reach into the cooler under the pastry and grab a stubby pint with a cardboard top and take that to the table with an empty glass. But now we have this big stainless dispenser that holds two five-gallon pails. Coming out of the bottom of each pail is a ten-inch rubber tube covered in a plastic sleeve to keep the tube clean as it's fed through a trigger operated by a heavy chrome handle. Once the pail is mounted properly the tube is cut off under the trigger so that all you have to do to get some milk is lift the heavy chrome handle. Instant cow, even more transparent now behind this spotless box of shiny metal.

The convenience of being able to switch cans when one runs out is impressive only when someone remembers to replace the empty. But when someone forgets and suddenly it's Christmas Day, Palm Dairies is closed and Dad has to phone Mr. Borch who's just now carving his turkey but will be right there Freddy, as soon as he can, then Dad looks at that gleaming hunk of modernity, shakes his head and curses the absence of both milk and memory.

Don't cut your food up all at once.

You've got to learn to eat properly. Scrub your nails. Flush the toilet. You be home by eight o'clock. Can't you do what I tell you? You'd better get busy and shine your dad's shoes or he'll tan your hide. Look at all the dirt you've tracked in. I do nothing but keep house for you day in and day out and what thanks do I get? You come home late at night and then you're off to some damned game or other the next day without even telling me. Don't I get any help around here?

Voice neither a scream nor a tight whisper. More like a yell. And then when she's really at the end of her rope she'll break down and cry. That's the hardest.

BETTER WATCH OUT FOR THE CRAW, BETTER WATCH

out for the goat. That's the mix, the breed, the half-breed, metis, quarter-breed, trace-of-a-breed true demi-semi-ethnic polluted rootless living technicolour snarl to complicate the underbelly panavision of racism and bigotry across this country. I know, you're going to say, that's just being Canadian. The only people who call themselves Canadian live in Ontario and have national sea-to-shining-sea twenty-twenty CPR vision.

When I was in elementary school we had to fill out a form at the beginning of each year. The first couple of years I was really confused. The problem was the blank after Racial Origin. I thought, well, this is Canada, I'll put down Canadian. But the teacher said no Freddy, you're Chinese, your racial origin is Chinese, that's what your father is. Canadian isn't a racial identity. That's turned out to be true. But I'm not really Chinese either. Nor were some of the other kids in my class *real* Italian, Doukhobor, or British.

Quite a soup. Heinz 57 Varieties. There's a whole bunch of us who've grown up as resident aliens, living in the hyphen. Like the Chinese kids who came over after 1949 couldn't take me into their confidence. I always ended up playing on the other team, against them, because they were foreign and I was white enough to be on the winning team. When I visited China and I told the guide of our tour group that I was Chinese he just laughed at me. I don't blame him. He, for all his racial purity so characteristic of mainland Chinese, was much happier thinking of me as a Canadian, something over there, white, Euro. But not Chinese.

That could be the answer in this country. If you're pure anything you can't be Canadian. We'll save that name for all the mixed bloods in this country and when the cities have Heritage Days and ethnic festivals there'll be a group that I can identify with, the Canadians. When the government gives out money for cultural centres we'll get ours too. These real Canadians could gain a legitimate marginalized position. The French-Canadians would have to be Quèbècois, the Mennonites Mennonite, Brits Brit. And if you're a Scot from Hamilton or a Jew from Winnipeg, then be that; I don't care.

But stop telling me what I'm not, what I can't join, what I can't feel or understand. And don't whine to me about maintaining your ethnic ties to the old country, don't explain the concept of time in terms of a place called Greenwich, don't complain about not being able to find Tootsie Rolls or authentic Mexican food north of the 49th.

Sometimes I'd rather be left alone.

and all that old-stuff China. As far as Grampa Wah was concerned his wife and her family could have whatever money he still had left, that and the small chunk of land that he'd bought and paid for. Let them farm it forever; he wasn't interested in that kind of life. Or, he told her, she could go with him if she wanted to, though he knew they probably wouldn't let her in anyway. She'd never leave Kaiping and her family, especially now that she'd become a landowner. But they would be o.k.; he would send money back when he struck it big again.

He returned to Canada in 1904, after four years back in China, enough time to get a wife and have three children. He had used up all the money he had made in Canada so he wanted to get back there and try his luck again. He told his wife that he was going to the Philippines but he knew there were better chances in Canada. The head tax had been raised twice since he left and he thought if he didn't get back to Canada soon it might be too expensive for him.

First he came to Vancouver but they had lots of laws there against Chinamen so he couldn't get much work. Since he didn't have a bunch of money to play the horses like the last time, he drifted out to the prairies, to Moose Jaw. He knew Henry Chow was there in a partnership in a restaurant with three other guys. Henry told him that no one wanted to sell out right away so he should wait awhile. He washed dishes for twenty-five dollars a month, fourteen to sixteen hours a day. Every night he had to wash the floor in the kitchen by using a potato sack under his knees and brushes in his hands.

At harvest time he got a job cooking on the CPR line that went all the way to Prince Albert. He'd work two days straight with one day off and they paid him forty dollars a month. But in the winter he went back to Moose Jaw and worked in the restaurant. All the partners and seven or eight other guys stayed there. It was warm and there was no work anywhere, so they all looked after the cafe.

One day Henry told him about a fellow in Swift Current who wanted to sell his share in the cafe. So he went down there to see about it. This guy was going back to China to get married, so he was selling. Lee Lung was the only other partner and Grampa knew one of Lee's uncles in the village next to his back in China. He had been lucky in gambling lately so he had five hundred dollars to put in. A few shares in a couple of cafes, he thought, and he could start to take it easy, let his money do the work.

The Venice Cafe worked out well. They made good profits because there were only two of them. So in 1906 he sold out some of his share to a few of Lee Lung's relatives and became a silent partner. He bought a working share in the Regal Cafe and by then his English was better so he worked up front, which was easier than the kitchen. He got to know a lot of the white guys and once in awhile he'd play cards with them. Except for a brief venture in Medicine Hat in 1912 he stayed in Swift Current. The Regal was really his main cafe for a long time, right into the thirties. But early on that's where he met his white wife, Florence.

$\mathcal{F}$LORENCE WAS THE CASHIER
AT THE REGAL. GOOD

with money. A young girl, serious, and a hard worker. Her family lived just down the street, across from the railway station. Her father and her brothers all worked on the CPR. They weren't farmers. Some people in town said she shouldn't work there. They didn't like white girls working in restaurants. This was just before Saskatchewan made a law against hiring white women to work in Chinese places.

But she was charmed by the dashing Jim Wah and, without better prospects, they got married in 1907. By the time the war came they had two girls and two boys. He not only continued to send money back to China but also, in 1916, sent a couple of the kids back to China. Florence was mad at him for that and never forgave him.

That caper convinced her that he was the devil, a gambler and a womanizer. She pulled in her outrage, anchored her lower lip, started to hide away money to get her children back, and joined the Salvation Army. I don't believe she smiled again in her lifetime, and who can blame her. That bastard.

*L*UCKY JIM ALWAYS HAD A BIG GOLD-TOOTHED SMILE

for everyone. He was a gambler, though not as hooked on it as some Chinese I've known. To have a grandfather named Lucky Jim, a spiffy dresser who sported a gold nugget stickpin and diamond cufflinks, a man of some reputation, was, I thought, pretty intriguing. But I didn't know, then, the sorrow he brought on my grandmother because of his gambling. To her, and I think most of the women in his family, he was a bit of a bastard.

He worked as a cook on the CPR when he came to Canada in 1892 and then for awhile as a cook on the boats around the West Coast. He struck it big at the race track in Vancouver which is what financed his brief but amorous return to China. When he came back to Canada in 1904, alone, he got into the cafe business as an investment for his winnings.

I never saw him work much in the cafe like his sons had to, but by the time I was old enough to know him he was already an old man. Always dapper with a gold nugget stickpin in his tie. I'd see him in the cafe playing the Chinese lottery, a bunch of mysterious red, green, and purple Chinese writing in little boxes in a pad of blotchy paper. He'd always say he wanted to get an eight spot and then do a kind of click-click at the corner of his mouth with his tongue and his teeth. Eight spot! he'd say, and laugh with his eyes and teeth full of gold. You could tell he was attracted to living the spiffy life. When he'd see us kids all dressed up, for Sunday school or a Chinese banquet or something, he'd always laugh and shout out at us, high muckamuck, eh?

But he didn't drink and it seemed to me he was always good to people, especially us kids, candy and jingly-jangly change fisted out of his pocket. Every New Year he would wrap quarters in red paper and put them in a bowl and we'd each get one for good luck.

He outlived his younger Canadian wife by a dozen years and, during his last years, was shuffled around amongst our family. One day I found him singing what were, according to my dad, Chinese nursery rhymes. He sat alone on the front porch and he had tears in his eyes. My mom said he was going senile. Finally he had to be put in an old folks' home. There the nurses complained about how he'd try to lift their skirts with his cane, how they couldn't understand him, how he'd say dirty things to them, how he'd try to catch them with that smile in his eyes, all dressed up and clean-shaven with no where to go, a troublemaker, that one, a yellow peril, an Amor de Cosmos Pariah, a Celestial, a John A. Macdonald mongrel, an Onderdonk question mark, a Royal Commission cuckoo, an Asiatic Exclusion League problem, a huckster, a leper, a depraved opium addict, a slant-eyed devil, a Mongolian, a heathen, bone-scraping ghoul, a pest, a wanton Cyprian, a Chinkie-Chinkie Chinaman, a nignog, an Ishmaelite, a cooley, a yellow belly—just another hungry ghost, just another last spike.

$\mathcal{H}$ow to Beat the Game (but first we'll take the nation. ♠

♠ If anything were lacking to show the negro's adaptability to American citizenship, his innate love of poker would settle the question. Too much praise can not be bestowed upon those negroes who have progressed from adject slavery to 'craps' to complete emancipation by poker. And I seriously believe that poker affords the only gate-way to full social and political recognition of the race. Take the Chinese question, for example. Does one suppose the Geary bill, prohibiting Chinese immigration, would ever have passed into law had the Mongolians taken kindly to poker? It was not fear of the introduction of idolotry by these heathens that impelled the congress of the United States to set up a fence against them. To be sure, that was the alleged reason, but members of congress who pushed the measure, and succeeded in having it placed upon the statute books, afterwards confessed that they had been spurred to action mainly by the assertions of the lobbyists that until Chinese immigration was speedily checked, 'fan tan' would inevitably supplant our national game. And hence the Geary law (after the order of the Monroe doctrine) stands as a sort of notice to the world that immigration which might retard the growth of our poker industry, is not wanted in this free country. (from *How to Beat the Game* by Garrett Brown, 1903)

𝓕AKING IT FROM ALL THAT LANGUAGE, IN THE

cafes (those brown-skinned men pinch me and talk in Chinese not to me but to the mysterious guttural nine-toned air by the big maple chopping block in the kitchen) and then hear my father speak from out of his/our mouth these same words with an axe to the edge of them, him with command and authority because he's smart, he's the boss, and he can scorn their playfulness, I think it is, their naiveté, because his mouth can move with dexterity between these men-sounds, between these secret sounds we only hear in the kitchen of the Elite or in the silent smoke-filled Chinese store, between these dense vocables of nonsense, and English, which is everywhere, at the front of the cafe, on the street, and at home. And that he does this alone, that no one else can move between these two tongues like he does, that puts him at the centre of our life, with more pivot to the world than anyone I know.

At home English is my mother love with laughing and "Just Mary" on CBC and big red volumes of *Journeys Through Bookland* and at supper when we see him he often makes a little slip of tongue, an accent which we think twice about correcting and at least a quick glance before laughing at, sometimes with him, but watch out for his quick dagger defense, you smart-aleck kids, you think you know so much, you don't know anything, you go to school but you're not so high muckamuck, and that'll be the redness in his face the English problem, him exposed.

Sometimes my mother's parents talk Swedish in front of me but they only use it to argue, and my mother's been to school so she speaks only English. Finally she can only understand the Swedish but no longer converse in it. By the time she meets my dad she has been half-erased and her English is good, it's blond.

*M*Y FATHER PLAYS MAH-JONG AND FAN-TAN.

While living in Trail, we drive over to Nelson one weekend and late at night we end up parked on Lake Street beside an old wooden building in the city's small Chinatown. Mom sits in the car with us kids, trying to get us to go to sleep. From the open second-floor window just above the car and the canopy of maple trees, we can hear the click-clack of the jade and ivory mah-jong pieces being shuffled over the table and the punctuative challenges and curses of the men playing the game. My mom's mad that my dad keeps playing so late because we still have a long drive back to Trail and I think she's worried that he'll lose a bundle.

But then even my mom plays mah-jong for awhile, in the afternoon over at Sue Kaiway's house with some of the Chinese women who have arrived after the Exclusion act is repealed.

During the fifties my parents play a lot of canasta, that doubledecked card game that is all the rage with its neat plastic mechanical shuffler. They only play poker as part of a family game when we play Rumoli. My sister still has the fold-up card table that I painted a Rumoli board on as a kid. It's a game we can all have fun with and it's where I learn most about gambling from my dad; how to bet, bluff, and laugh.

Blackjack table at the fall fair, late at night, Jimmy Gee, one thousand dollars, ten thousand dollars. My dad says Jimmy's addicted. Lots of Chinamen are. Crazy.

*W*HEN I SIT ON ONE OF THE STOOLS

at the front counter and survey the serving area I see, along that front wall of the cafe, to the right of the big front window, a landscape of stainless steel soda fountain, pastel green Beach milkshake carousel with its semi-circle of five beaters (only ever seen four going at once), Campbell's soup rack and heater, big double-can milk dispenser (the kind with the rubber tubing that spurts all over the counter when you cut it), coolers and pastry display cases, and, finally, before the booths begin, the large stainless coffee urns with glass tubes: three spigots, two coffee and one hot water—steaming. Underneath the display cases the coolers for the pitchers of juice, a large bowl of butter patties in ice-water, and a cloth whipping cream dispenser (cone shaped with a cake-decorating nipple at one end). The doors to these coolers are smaller-sized replicas of the thick kitchen cooler door, same kind of hardware that closes with a nice hollow and metallic snap.

Behind the sliding glass doors of the display cabinet, each patty of butter is ready to serve on a separate tiny dish in the cafe's dish pattern of plain white with a yellow and blue curlicue. Before each rush hour we make up several trays of butter patties. The patties themselves are cut up in a special butter cutter in the kitchen, a job I like to be given, not just because of the precision of the cutter, but because I have to be in the kitchen, and can hover, if only for a few minutes, within the meaningless but familiar hum of Cantonese and away from all the angst of the arrogant white world out front.

In the top display cases are the pies (apple, raisin, lemon, chocolate cream, coconut cream, and the three-inch-high Boston cream). There's also a tray of miniature cream jugs, filled and ready to grab for the next rush.

On the counter space in front of the glass display case are trays of sugar doughnuts, butterhorns, and butter tarts. Lots of my friends come in after school and have a Coke and a butter tart or a brown cow (chocolate milk) and a doughnut (sugar or jelly).

The metal tracks of the glass door sliders often get gungy with food and grease so on a Sunday afternoon shift I lift out the glass doors and clean the tracks with a knife. The next day the new waitress goes to close it on the run during the lunch hour rush and it slides like silk so smooth and fast that the plate glass shatters when it hits and there are glass beads in all the cream pies, butter and Jell-O and she stops dead in her tracks stunned hands full with four dishes of deep-apple pie and looks at the frown on my dad's brown face, a young girl red with the thought that she's just blown her new job until Mrs. Morrison steamrollers in with a broom and a jesus christ, lassie, get on with ya, I'll clean it up! bobbing and weaving in and out of the rest of us running through the mess with our orders listening to Mrs. Morrison curse to no one in particular that the friggin' help around here could all stand a bit more head on their shoulders and what the hell are we gonna do for desserts now somebody'd better check in the kitchen and see if Seto's got any extra fer chrisake watch out where yer goin whyncha just wait'll I get this mess off the floor before you go trackin glass all over the blessed cafe!

$\mathcal{I}$N NELSON MY FATHER JOINS
THE LIONS CLUB,

one of those service clubs like the Rotary Club, Gyros, and Junior Chamber of Commerce. And that's what most of the clubs are for, business connections, working on community projects, and having some fun. Most of the clubs meet at the Hume Hotel for lunch or dinner once a week and each meeting is full of shenanigans, like having to pay a fine for not wearing a tie and things like that. My dad really enjoys the Lions Club and works hard on projects, like coaching Little League baseball and putting on the mid-summer bonspiel pancake breakfast on Baker Street. I think what he likes most, though, is the kidding around, the high jinks.

I think a lot of his kidding around is in order to hide his embarrassment at not knowing English as well as he'd like to. His only schooling in English he picks up during six months in Cabri, Saskatchewan, just north of Swift Current. His father sends him there to work in a small cafe soon after he returns from China. And then one of his sisters, Hanna, helps him out with reading and writing a bit during those first years back with his English-speaking family. Whatever else he learns about English he picks up from working in the cafe.

When he joins the Lions Club and has to give an initiation speech, he gets my mother to help him write something up. She says he's very nervous about this event; worried that he might flub it, make a fool of himself, the only Chinaman at an all-white dinner meeting. But there he is, with his little speech on a piece of paper in front of all these Baker Street nickel millionaires in the Hume Hotel dining room, thanking these guys for inviting him to join their club, thanking them for making Nelson such a wonderful place to live and raise his family, and then thanking them for this meal with the wonderful *sloup*. We always kid around at home when he says *sloup* and he laughs and, we suspect, even says it that way intentionally just to horse around with us. But here such a slip just turns him copper red (the colour you get when you mix yellow with either embarrassment or liquor). So when he hears himself say *sloup* for soup he stops suddenly and looks out at the expected embarrassed and patronizing smiles from the crowd. Then he does what he has learned to do so well in such instances, he turns it into a joke, a kind of self put-down that he knows these white guys like to hear: he bluffs that Chinamen call soup *sloup* because, as you all know, the Chinese make their cafe soup from the slop water they wash their underwear and socks in, and besides, it's just like when you hear me eating my soup, Chinamen like to slurp and make a lot of noise. That's a compliment to the cook!

So he fakes it, and I guess I pick up on that sense of faking it from him, that English can be faked. But I quickly learn that when you fake language you see, as well, how everything else is a fake.

QUITE SUDDENLY LO BOK

REAPPEARS IN MY LIFE.

For years after leaving home I've had a craving for some Chinese food taste that I haven't been able to pin down. An absence that gnaws at sensation and memory. An undefined taste, not in the mouth but down some blind alley of the mind. The other day I was shopping in a Chinese food market and got curious about a large mound of Chinese white turnips. I couldn't remember having anything like it at our dinner table, thinking of the mashed yellow rutabagas in western food. It's obviously popular amongst the Chinese, for the pile of phallic brassica was being rapidly picked over. I asked a woman standing beside me on the edge of the crowd if she could tell me how the vegetable was used. She described the dish and I knew instantly I had found a lost taste.

Buy a good sized Chinese white turnip, or lo bok. Even Safeway will sometimes carry them. Start the dish by washing and setting aside to soak about a tablespoon of small, dried shrimp. Peel the turnip and cut it up into french-fry-sized strips. Blanch by bringing to a boil and then take out and pour cold water over. Slice and stir-fry some beef with garlic and soy sauce. You can use a little onion if you want to (my mother doesn't). Strain the cooled turnips and add them to the stir-fry along with the shrimp and the water it's been soaking in. Simmer in the liquid until the turnip just starts to soften. Add a little more water if necessary and serve thin that way or thicken with a little corn starch. During cooking the lo bok turns from white to a light taupe. The taste roots itself as a miscegenated bitterness of soil and ocean transfused by the dark brown soya into guttural pungency.

SITKUM DOLLAH GRAMPA WAH
LAUGHS AS HE FLIPS

a shiny half-dollar coin into the air. I say tails and he laughs too bad Freddy and shows me the head of King George the sixth. Then he puts a quarter into my hand, closes his brown and bony hand over mine, pinches my cheek while he says you good boy Freddy, buy some candy!

Whenever I hear grampa talk like that, high muckamuck, sitkum dollah, I think he's sliding Chinese words into English words just to have a little fun. He has fun alright, but I now realize he also enjoys mouthing the dissonance of encounter, the resonance of clashing tongues, his own membership in the diasporic and nomadic intersections that have occurred in northwest North America over the past one hundred and fifty years.

I don't know, then, that he's using Chinook jargon, the pidgin vocabulary of colonial interaction, the code-switching talkee-talkee of the contact zone. ✣

The term grampa uses most is high muckamuck (from *hyu muck-amuck*, originally among First Nations meaning plenty to eat and

---

✣ Mary Louise Pratt describes this as the practice of

> *code-switching,* in which speakers switch spontaneously and fluidly between two languages. . . . In the context of fiercely monolingual dominant cultures like that of the United States, code-switching lays claim to a form of cultural power: the power to own but not be owned by the dominant language. Aesthetically, code-switching can be a source of great verbal subtlety and grace as speech dances fluidly and strategically back and forth between two languages and two cultural systems. Code-switching is a rich source of wit, humour, puns, word play, and games of rhythm and rhyme. " 'Yo soy la Malinche'," in *Twentieth Century Poetry: From Text to Context,* edited by Peter Verdonk, London: Routledge, 1993: 177.

then transformed, through the contact zone, into big shot, big-time operator). He exclaims high muckamuck whenever he sees us get into our best clothes for Sunday school. Or, even sometimes when he gets all spiffed up, arranging his hanky to pouf out of the breast pocket of his suit, angling his tie into a full Windsor, fixing his diamond cuff-links and shaking his arms so the shirt-sleeves will fill out smooth, sticking the gold nugget tie pin through the layers of tie and shirt, brushing some lint off of his trouser leg as he stands to reach up for his best felt hat, and then walking out the door with a twinkle in his eyes chuckling high muckamuck.

Though my grandfather seems to say the phrase with a kind of humorous and testy tone, my father translates high muckamuck into a term of class derision. He doesn't like pretension and, though he certainly works hard to raise our family up a middle-class notch, he'll sideswipe anyone he sees putting on airs or using class advantage.

Don't think you're such a high muckamuck, my dad said to me after my brother Ernie ratted on me driving down Baker Street in Dad's Monarch with my right arm around a girl. It's not class itself, really, but how you use it.

For example, he tears into one of the Baker Street nickel millionaires who picks up a tip from a booth that hasn't been cleaned yet. We all know the tip's there; it's at least a bill because you can see it sticking out from under a plate. As the guy's looking through the

---

Pratt's description of the "contact zone" is equally useful in considering the dynamics of foreignicity:

> The space of colonial encounters, the space in which peoples geographically and historically separated come into contact with each other and establish ongoing relations, usually involving conditions of coercion, radical inequality, and intractable conflict. . . ."Contact zone" . . . is often synonymous with "colonial frontier." But while the latter term is grounded within a European expansionist perspective (the frontier is a frontier only with respect to Europe), "contact zone" is an attempt to invoke the spatial and temporal copresence of subjects previously separated by geographic and historical disjunctures, and whose trajectories

menu my dad goes up to him and says jesus christ Murphy what do you think you're doing lifting the girls' tips. They work hard for that money and you got more'n you know what to do with. You think you're such a high muckamuck. You never leave tips yourself and here you are stealing small change. I want you to get out of here and don't come into this cafe again. The guy leaves, cursing at my dad, saying he doesn't know why anyone'd wanna eat this Chink food anyway. He never does come back. A pipsqueak trying to be high muckamuck.

And I only realize, right here on this page, when the cooks in the kitchen swear You mucka high! at me, they've transed the phrase out of their own history here. I thought they were swearing in Chinese.

Whenever my mother uses the term she adds a syllable by saying high mucketymuck.

---

now intersect. By using the term "contact," I aim to foreground the inter-active, improvisational dimensions of colonial encounters so easily ignored or sup-pressed by diffusionist accounts of conquest and domination. A "contact" per-spective emphasizes how subjects are constituted in and by their relations among colonizers and colonized ... not in terms of separateness or apartheid, but in terms of copresence, interaction, interlocking understandings and practices, often within radically asymmetrical relations of power. *Imperial Eyes: Travel Writing and Transculturation.* London: Routledge, 1992: 6-7.

See also Monica Kin Gagnon's catalogue essay on Henry Tsang's installation "Utter Jargon":

Chinook Jargon was developed initially as a pidgin language amongst west coast First Nations peoples. Used primarily for trade purposes, Chinook Jargon's (roughly) five-hundred word vocabulary can be more specifically traced to the dialect of the Columbia River Chinook with further influences from English, French and Nuu-chah-nulth (a language group located predominantly on the west coast of Vancouver Island). At the height of its usage, Chinook Jargon had an estimated one hundred thousand speakers throughout a region stretching from northern California to Alaska, and from the Rockies to the Pacific Ocean. As Tsang notes, the jargon was unable to resist the dominance of English, and fell out of use during the first half of the 1900s. *Dual Cultures,* Kamloops Art Gallery: Kamloops, 1993: 9.

*T*HE CHRISTMAS BEFORE HE
DIES HE COMES TO

Buffalo. We're graduate students there and I drive to Toronto to pick up him and Mom and Glenda, my little sister, from their cross-Canada train trip. A friend of mine has snapped a few tickets to a Leafs' game in the Gardens; he's excited by that. I take them to see Niagara Falls, but our car has no heater and it's about 15 below. He's intrigued by all the black people in Buffalo. We play cards a lot—hearts—and he really gets into it. But one night the game blows up because he misunderstands one of the rules. We all side against him and his ire rises. At times like that he's alone. You can see he knows he's wrong but defends himself in the face of it anyway. This playing with anger, with a double edge there, almost arithmetic, in that attractive way, some armature of temptation at work that urges on bravado and resistance—dead set.

$\mathcal{L}$AST CHRISTMAS WHEN I
GRABBED YOU BY THE

shoulders and shook you from so much anger welled up in me after days of frustration at your indecision and malaise the fire reaching into my eyes and mouth for you to smarten up and pay attention to our world, totally enraged there on the stairs at some little thing you'd said or not done, that, that was from that well deep within me and at least my father maybe his who knows now your anger too could be ours this pit of something having gone on but only surfacing like Ahab's whale unpredictably in a sudden eruption—not just being pissed off but all the way back to something not mine, something I brought with me from before the first angry scream at birth caught deep back in the throat despite me and now you have it too given to you probably in moments like that on the stairs fired up at just that crack in our father-daughter life you and I not seeing eye to eye Dog Star raging between us, that was something from our fathers and there I was your father giving it to you full force and you impotent in tears of shock at the physical. Just last Christmas. Those total pieces cored to the heart, whatever you think, rage to the skin's story is colour-deep, colour deep. Later in my life, or always, maybe even yours, this anger gram becomes the free-floating and yet forever-foreign im from migration.

THE LOTTERY, PAK KOP PIU, IS A HUB

of activity around the cafes. I'm intrigued and mystified by the game because it appears like magic out of my grampa's overcoat pocket (now you see it), as rows of green Chinese characters printed on a sheaf of cheap pulp paper bound by a string punched through the spine. Every day someone, either my grampa (now you don't) or some other Chinaman, comes into the cafe and sells chances at the lottery. Most of the kitchen and any Chinese out front, like my father, are eager to buy a chance. It's pretty cheap, just a few quarters. Even some of the waitresses and white customers are into it.

Winning brings out a slap-happy eight spot! from my grampa. That's his favourite good-luck expression and he even uses it when he horses around with us kids. He'll click to show his gold teeth and say to me, as he hands me some candy, eight spot, eh Freddy! Sometimes he'll give me some money, a quarter or a dollar, just because he won earlier in the day.

Whenever I'm there watching him when he's buying a lottery he'll get me to choose the characters and he marks each one confidently with a red dot, his eyes laughing, trusting me to come up with the winning combination. First born, for luck. And I'm a believer. Stars in our eyes.

WHY GRAMPA EATS SUCH MUCK,
OR DRINKS IT,

insists on it, I can't figure out. End of meal, homework, cleaning up the dishes, and there he sits, still at the table, while Mom or Dad gets his wet rice. Boiled burnt brown crust in the rice pot looks sludgy but smells sweet. Dad has it once in a while but not often. I try it a couple of times but don't like it. Going out of us. Gone now, from him, to him, to me. We aren't forced to eat it, as we are the salt fish, the ginger, the slimy sea weed. When he slurps his wet rice things get quiet, we don't have to think of all those starving people in China. Him though, his long grey side-hair slopped over his bald head old and shiny brown smacking his toothless chops, lifts his bowl for yet another. Authentic. Like health. Diuretic. Not pissed off. Not him. A great distance dwells in his face. Even when he walks into the cafe high muckamuck, his eyes smile through us, past us, to something else far away. I always think it's China, mysterious, something he knows and we don't. How taste remembers life. Sipping underneath that wet, burned rice after dinner in his gaze is some long night far away on the other side of earth in other eyes and other pots burned hot in the charcoal clay stove flickered light from the lit dry grass under the same stars fields of rice and water Pacific Ocean end of murmured sadness jumped intestinal interstices, bisected, circulated, tongue's track, crossed into gut, guttered now between the pages of this book the floating gaze and taste burnt right through to the spine.

RICE IS WHITE RICE, POLISHED, AND, IF COOKED

properly, should be just slightly sticky but not wet. Here's how my dad taught me when I left home and I discovered that I couldn't live without it.

Wash two to three cups (more is always better because you can use it later for a breakfast of fried rice and tofu) by swirling it in a heavy pot with your fingers and draining. Put enough water in to cover rice plus the thickness of your fingers as you hold them top-of-hand down on the rice (variation due to age, gender, race, or class is negligible—the results are always perfection). Bring to a boil then simmer with a heavy lid on for about half an hour.

If this is done properly you should have a crust of slightly burnt rice around the bottom and the sides of the pot. After scooping out the loose rice, put enough water in the pot to cover burnt rice and boil until this black and brown rice loosens and you have a dark-coloured soup that is sweet and can be eaten with relished meditation.

*D*ONNA MORI'S SHIFT STARTS
AT SEVEN.

Morning Fred, how's it going, as she ties her apron on. Gosh, still snowing, that'll make it hard for all the shoppers today.

Yeah, but it's still gonna be a busy one, everybody'll be downtown doing last-minute shopping. You do number nine and I'll finish off the counter. And take Shu a cup of coffee after you get old man Moore's toast.

She moves right into the traffic and now that she's on the move he feels the pressure ease a bit, only has to handle the counter customers and the till. Donna's snappy, cute, and smiles at all the customers. They love her. She works all the booths, cleans up the tables, and gets at little things like filling the tray of miniature cream jugs that go with each cup of coffee. With all the store clerks coming in just before opening, they're fairly busy and only talk small talk as they intersect at the coffee urn for a few seconds.

How's Connie?

Wonder if your dad and brothers'll come into town tomorrow?

Wow, look at George today, pretty hung over. I heard his wife kicked him out.

Did you win your curling game last night?

Fill those slyrups when you get a chance.

Pick up Bob's stack a hots for me will ya?

aFTER THE WAR, JAPANESE-CANADIANS
CONTINUE TO LIVE

scattered through the Kootenays in the places they've been interned, like Greenwood, Kaslo, and Slocan City. My father thinks highly of their tenacity and diligence. They're really hard workers, he says, and if we had a couple of those girls working in the cafe they'd be a hell of lot more reliable than these white girls who whine a lot and never show up for work.

Some Sundays we take a family drive to one of these small towns and dad will inquire in the local Chinese cafes about finding some JC girls to work at the Diamond. He eventually finds two girls who have finished school and are looking for work, up the valley in Slocan City. My father comes to some agreement with their father that the girls will work at the Diamond for wages and room and board. Miko and Donna Mori have their own rooms above the cafe and become an integral part of life in the cafe; almost family, as they say. Their father and brothers, all loggers, visit when they come down from Slocan City some Saturdays and my dad and Mr. Mori will sit in a booth at the back and talk.

The cooks in the cafe don't like it at first. Chinese have some animosity towards Japanese, my dad explains, because the Japanese occupied China. And, perhaps, one might read some resentment into the fact that the Chinese had been singled out for head tax and exclusion from immigration but not the Japanese. Miko and Donna, however, are such vivacious and likeable people that it doesn't take long for them to win the hearts of everyone in the cafe, particularly the customers who think they're Chinese anyway.

The older sister, Miko, works up front as cashier and her younger sister, Donna, turns out to be the best waitress the cafe has ever had—a real sparkplug my dad calls her. Donna is just a little older than me but we always have a lot of fun, joking around, flipping coins, playing the juke box. She gets more tips than anyone else so she always has a pocketful of change. She garners quite a large following of loyal customers who refuse to be waited on by anyone but her.

The three of us, one summer weekend, take the bus to Spokane and Donna and I see five movies in a row, from noon until nearly midnight. I fall in love with Grace Kelly in *High Noon* and Donna falls in love with Gene Kelly in *Singing in the Rain*. Small-town kids, big city Tootsie Roll modern movie America fifties. Lots of Coke and popcorn. Donna gets a new pair of saddle loafers and I get a new pair of runners at Sears-Roebuck. We do the whole trip on tips.

𝒯HE BEST TIMES IN THE DIAMOND ARE AROUND

Christmas. We bring boxes of decorations up from the basement—
stringers, lights, tinsel, red paper balls, and so forth. The cafe is
rather narrow and the only place for the tree is on top of the now-
silent big green air conditioner. We all have a hand in the decorat-
ing. Every time there's a lull we do a little. Across the big front window I spray stencilled white snowflakes, a few reindeer, and the
letters N-O-E-L in an arc over a manger scene. In the corner of the
window behind the cashier is a poster advertising the Diamond's
Christmas Day and New Year's Day special dinners at a dollar
eighty-five per plate and noting a closing time of eight o'clock for
those days and eves.

At Christmas the cafe really buzzes. And I don't think anyone's
spirit runs higher than my dad's. He's ebullient when he welcomes
customers and laughs shiftily as he spikes the coffee of the boys from
the Timber Club. Even on Christmas Day, though he has to open up
at six in the morning for the CPR shift workers and the rooming
house people, he gets us up an hour before he has to leave, about four
a.m., to open our presents. He doesn't want to miss a thing.

New Year's is also a big time, especially for the Chinese. Even
though January first isn't the real Chinese New Year, all the cooks
still say Goong Hey Fa Choy, and us kids are expected to say it back.

Above the large booth at the back of the cafe we hang up and
plug in the feature decoration, a large sign of a winter scene done in
glued-on glitter and featuring a blinking light bulb behind a large
diamond framed by a red-and-blue ribbon that reads, *Season's
Greetings from the Diamond Grill.*

*M*Y DAD HALF JOKES
ONCE IN AWHILE THAT

I should look for a good Chinese wife. Of course he'll say that more to get a rise out of my mom than really mean it. I think.

The only Chinese girl I ever swoon for is an older girl, from Vancouver. A couple of summers she stays with her aunt and uncle across the street from us. She agrees to give my brothers and me some Chinese lessons and I wait for her on our back steps every morning. She's tall and beautiful with long black hair, red lipstick, and likes to joke around.

But in the early fifties there aren't too many Chinese girls in sight. If anyone brings kids over from China it's often a paper son, a teenager with subsistence guaranteed by distant friends or relatives. Anyway, most of the Chinese girls are brought over for men already here.

Most of the Chinese women I know, the older ones from China, seem kind of lazy. They just stay home and get their daughters-in-law to do the housework. At least that's what my mom and dad say. And they never smile very much. I know I don't want a wife who's going to turn out to be indolent and stern.

You'd think, having grown up in China, my father would marry one of those girls you can arrange to bring over, instead of a Swedish girl from Swift Current. Neither of his brothers marry Chinese either.

a FEW YEARS AGO
I CAME UPON SOME

of my Granny Wah's family photos. Pictures of her Canadian-born Scottish mother, her Irish-born father, and her Scots grandfather. That would be my great-great-grandfather, taken nearly one hundred years ago, swooped into Canada, hungry for his land of god-given rights and Canadian Pacific opportunity.

In the photo, he looks to be just a little older than I am now. A long white beard and a full mane of white hair. His eyes are penetrating northern rivets and a little Mongolian-looking squint, as some Scots are prone to have. Visage a bit of a stern scowl and you get the feeling he's had to put up with a certain amount of silent indignation. Not pissed off, but righteous, inheritor of his railroad earth.

And no head tax either!

*S*ALISBURY STEAK, A PATTY OF
GROUND BEEF MIXED

with various seasonings and boiled or fried, is named after J. H. Salisbury, a nineteenth-century English nutritionist.

Salisbury steak at the Diamond Grill, as cooked by Shu Ling Mar, seems so much more than mere hamburger. Shu's patty is oblong, about the size of a sirloin, and he serves it with mashed potatoes, gravy, and fried onions. It really is a poor man's steak. Lots of the day-shift workers from the CPR have it for supper. I know Mr. Carrier, who drives the coal delivery truck and speaks English with a French accent, comes in every Saturday afternoon at four-thirty for his Salisbury steak. He always has a chocolate sundae for dessert instead of the Jell-O or rice pudding or custard that comes with the meal, so instead of the regular price of a dollar twenty-five his bill comes to a dollar sixty. I've never seen any of the Maple Leaf hockey players who come in here have Salisbury though. They always have real steaks, and french fries. And, while Shu would be angry if he caught any of us ordering a real steak for our meal, he doesn't mind once in awhile if we order a Salisbury, particularly on Sundays. The combination of gravy and onions with the beef makes this one of my favourites; a really straight meal with a slight cachet of class and masculinity.

I'M JUST A BABY, MAYBE SIX MONTHS (.5%)

old. One of my aunts is holding me on her knee. Sitting on the ground in front of us are her two daughters, 50% Scottish. Another aunt, the one who grew up in China with my father, sits on the step with her first two children around her. They are 75% Chinese. There is another little 75% girl cousin, the daughter of another 50% aunt who married a 100% full-blooded Chinaman (full-blooded, from China even). At the back of the black-and-white photograph is my oldest boy cousin; he's 25% Chinese. His mother married a Scot from North Battleford and his sisters married Italians from Trail. So there, spread out on the stoop of a house in Swift Current, Saskatchewan, we have our own little western Canadian multicultural stock exchange.

We all grew up together, in Swift Current, Calgary, Trail, Nelson and Vancouver (27% of John A's nation) and only get together now every three years (33%) for a family reunion, to which between 70% and 80% of us show up. Out of fifteen cousins only one (6.6%) married a 100% pure Chinese.

The return on these racialized investments has produced colourful dividends and yielded an annual growth rate that now parallels blue-chip stocks like Kodak and Fuji, though current global market forces indicate that such stocks, by their volatile nature, will be highly speculative and risky. Unexpected developments (like Immigration Acts) could knock estimates for a loop. Always take future projections with either a grain of salt or better still a dash of soy.

$\mathcal{C}$OURSE AGAIN, NOW, WE'RE TALKING
A DIFFERENT GENERATION,

an older cousin explains to me as we sit breezing around a picnic table at a Wah family reunion. Now, we're talking half Chinese. And, I don't know if it's the environment, the upbringing, the small-pox, what—Ethel and your dad looked more Chinese than anybody, although I think my own mother covered it up with makeup, plucked her eyebrows, lipstick, rouge, the works. She was pretty wild, going out a lot to dances and stuff like that. But there are pic-tures of Lil when she was a young girl where probably she looks the most Chinese of all the kids.

But Flo was of a quieter nature and I think there wasn't any choice for her. She either had to be wilder and go with the white boys or be accepted and marry a Chinaman. And so she did and Poppa fixed it up with Roy for her.

So now this younger generation isn't even half. We're all chipped up into quarters and thirds and eighths and most of the kids you can't tell what they are except their names. Chow, Freschi, Gee, Prysiaznuk, Yee, D'Andrea, Leier, Lyon, Wah. Never know they're all cousins.

$\mathcal{W}$HAT ANIMA GETS THROUGH
THE FAMILY GHOSTS IMMEDIATE

meditation taken to each chakra as hand holds out a stubble of language, body alone and pissed off?

Chan didn't really want to come over here. He says: my uncle paid for a paper. I thought I'd try it out for a few months and then go back. My father and another uncle were already here; they had a place up in Kamloops. The guy who signed me as his son came from San Francisco. I almost didn't make it because there were some contradictions in our statements. But we hired a good lawyer and he made it work. I only came here with a piece of paper and I've stayed, but I'm not rich. And if I want a wife it looks like I'll have to go back home.

What avalanche of news synaptic snaps renumbers days and places as a gambled problem poses plot down through the family midden?

When Leung made his claim at immigration, he said he only had one wife and one son. That made it easier to get in. He says: if I told them about the whole family, parents, seven brothers, two sisters, my own daughters, they would have made the interrogation much harder because they would be worried about twenty or thirty more later on.

What about Sweden and Scotland and Ireland and Ontario? Or even Pender and Main some spring Sunday morning, quiet, on the way to the Vancouver train station 1916–1966? Bottomed? Oceaned?

The whole country, Canada, the States, everywhere, Europeans. At the same time Chinese were prevented from coming here, white families, sons and daughters and everybody, could get boat passage and even more. The government wanted those people to come here so badly they even offered land. As if that fold in the tectonic plate along the west coast was like a crack where the yellow peril could sneak in.

What about her who can offer nothing more than inherited impossible structures made up from no scratch?

Rosie Lee came here in the twenties, a time when the only women who could get in were the wives of wealthy merchants or prostitutes. Rosie was bought from her family by a guy in Hong Kong who said he wanted to take her to Canada with him. He made her disguise herself as a man by braiding her hair and dressing her up in man's clothes; she wore the black cap that Chinese men still wore, like a beanie. The guy had bribed the immigration official in Victoria so they didn't inspect her too closely. He paid the Head Tax and then she had to work as a prostitute for the many overseas Chinese labourers hanging out in Victoria and Vancouver who would never be able to afford a wife. That's why she owns three cafes and a hotel; she never married, but she was a good gambler too and made a lot of money over the years.

She turns, over Saskatchewan, a large mother of place and love but bitter.

Neither of my grandmothers ever learned to drive a car. They came out of northern Europe through eastern Canada to the whisper-dry prairies. I don't know if they ever had mushrooms to cook with but they were always cooking something. One cooked soda biscuits and one cooked yinger snaps. One drank tea and one drank coffee. They hardly ever smiled but when they did they were indoors.

He, his eyes sparkle, brown finger with long, slim nail points to the green spot eight spot and he smiles gold teeth as he takes his lottery book out of an overcoat pocket and slaps the worn pages on the cafe counter. He laughs and his eyes glitter, water.

Ontogeny recapitulates phylogeny. A handful of dead toenails. When the deep purple falls.

Any more imprint shadowed on the psychic rose? Pea inside the pod?

$\mathcal{T}$HE WAH FAMILY REUNIONS ARE
USUALLY DURING THE

long weekend in August and we sit around in mid-afternoon with a
few drinks. I ask Ray, my oldest boy cousin, about the move to Trail,
B.C., and the Italian connection:

We knew nobody in Trail. Did I ever tell you this story, when we
came down that Smelter hill, in an old Hudson, Mom had less than
two dollars.

But why Trail of all places?

Because there was a rumour in Calgary that you could get a job
in Trail. So we came down the hill and drove into downtown Trail
and Mom bought a loaf of bread and a package of baloney, and we
drove up the gulch and up through the tunnel at Anabel and pulled
off to the side of the road, beside a little field. Mom was going to
make some sandwiches for us, and there was an old guy there that
had a flat tire, and Dad helped him fix it, and he asked us where we
were staying so we told him our story and he said drive back down
the gulch, he told us approximately how far to go, and look up on
the hillside and you'll see this big orange building, and that's Lady
Chapella's place and she'll give you a room. It was partly furnished,
it was two rooms, kitchen, dining room, and a big bedroom. It had
two beds and some plates. We just had what we had in the car, those
were all our worldly possessions, and that's where we got a room and
she said Dad could go downtown and get some groceries, go down
to Tony Tonelli's and tell him you're here to get a job and he'll give
you some groceries. And Dad went up to CM&S next day and there
was no job. So we waited for about a week, and Dad had been doing
some roofing, he'd tarred some roofs, anyway he got on a week later
and he started tarring roofs. And Mom went to work at CM&S, I

think she worked at Warfield. Women mopped floors and did cleanup jobs, the two of them were working up there.

But they did alright and years later, after they got into the Dollar Cleaners, Dad got a chance to buy the building, get into some more debt. Over the years Dad pissed more money away on financing, which was the only way to go if you didn't have a pot to piss in to start with. But then that dry cleaners raised a lot of kids. And all the money Dad pissed away on cars, Buicks, remember him buying new cars all the time, maybe one a year.

Yeah, Uncle Andy had to have his new car.

Roadmaster Buicks, christ! A few DeSotos in between.

A lot of the family came out from the prairies after your mom and dad.

It seemed to be that to get ahead you had to come out west. We had kinda got slotted, I don't know, our lots were already chosen for us on the prairies. There was no way to get ahead on real estate, the restaurants were already established, the old Chinese partners were all there, had their shares in the cafes, and it was hard to break away from. And the prairies were going downhill.

And then one of the smart-aleck kids who's hanging around our picnic table in the shade laughs and says hey Uncle Ray, how can something as flat as the prairies be on a hill? Har, har, har!

Listen you little bugger, those were tough times. Saskatchewan had been hit pretty hard. If we hadn't got out of there you'd just be a hayseed.

And then Ray laughs, shit, that big hill coming down from the smelter is the first hill I ever saw; it's stamped on my mind forever. All of Trail has its eyes up that hill. You either get a job on the hill for the rest of your life, like Satch here, or you gotta get out of there. It's done our family pretty good. How do you think you kids would have got your cars and been able to play around, if it hadn't been for the hill?

$\mathcal{W}$HENEVER WE ASK AUNTY
ETHEL ABOUT CHINA OR

about her father who sent her to China as a nine-year-old big sister to young Freddy, she just gives a sneer. She doesn't want to talk about it. Nearly eighty years later she still feels her life's outrage. She's long outlived two husbands (both of convenience, to them and her father, not her) and all but the youngest of her six brothers and sisters. At our family reunions she's the eldest, the queen. She's had a harder life than most of us, tenaciously sustaining her family of three boys and two girls without the help of her husbands; indeed, despite their liabilities. She sees through everyone, particularly the men. Him lazy boy, she'll observe about someone's spoiled son. Her too fat! She'll laugh at a bit of horseplay, but she pretty much remains silent, especially when we ask her about China.

So when Aunty Ethel shows the anger she's carried all these years, all the resentment for the roles she's been forced to accept, for the curve she was thrown as a young girl being sent to China, for the men (none as strong as she, yet commissioned by her father to own her), for the slavish servitude to her Chinese stepmother and stepsisters, for her father's filial Confucianism and neglect at leaving her alone in China, for a languagelessness impossible to overcome for a woman, thus, for the imposed interruptions and silences of a life so totally intended by others that she can only outlive them all, when her body shrugs against this perpetual masculine writing of her memory and her history, who can blame her for the scornful glance and sad harumph that glances back.

Us go now, she'll say when she's had enough.

THEY'RE OLD AND SITTING ON THE COUCH AND

he has his arm around her. He's still fairly lean and spiffy, wears a tie, a knowing pleased curve to his lips. Their right hands are clasped and rest on his knee.

She looks frumpy and stooped, caved in, quite tired, and her mouth curves the opposite from his, downward.

He's a Chinaman; did he do this to her? Her father an Irishman; did he do this to her?

Her sadness so large, her left hand rolling the hem of her dress, still turns, over Saskatchewan, our grandmother of place and onward Christian soldiers with love, but bitter love.

$\mathcal{W}$HEN ETHEL BROKE HER HIP,
IN MOOSE JAW,

Ray explains, Poppa and I went out there. She was running this rooming house all by herself (her husband Chow was dead then). She was alone with the kids and broke her hip and couldn't run the place anymore, so we took the train out there from Calgary. That's when I remember Poppa doing the cooking, cuz he fed me royally. He used to steam pork all the time with bean curd paste on it, one of my favourite dishes.

I make it by chopping up about a cup of shoulder or loin pork. Make sure it's lean. And then you mix up about a tablespoon of bean curd paste, you know, that red, spicy stuff you can get in a jar in Chinatown, along with a little soy sauce, maybe one to two teaspoons, a pinch of sugar, and—Poppa never did it, I think I picked it up from your dad—a couple shots of brandy or whiskey. Combine this with the meat and steam cook until the pork is done, about fifteen minutes.

You know what I like to have with this, besides a bowl of rice? Some of those bitter greens; I don't know what you call them, really dark green.

*A*FTER OUR FAMILY MOVES
OUT TO BRITISH COLUMBIA

in 1943, my grandmother on my Chinese side, the Scots-Irish one from Ontario, periodically takes several of us cousins back to the prairies for summer holidays. We stay with a variety of relatives still living in Swift Current. After a couple of weeks, always sooner than we expect, she puts us on the train and takes us back to Trail and Nelson complaining that she knows when and where she isn't wanted. Her stew, as they say, has been stirred. She just sits in her train seat and looks grim and pouty. She has a large lower lip, as many of us after her have, and this exaggerates her smouldering. I hope my daughters, who also have full lower lips, don't have to carry her kind of ire. They need to let their gorges rise; we all do, need to channel our granny's grammar.

Cook your silence, but don't let it simmer.

WELL, RAY, THE OTHER
QUESTION I'M KIND OF

interested in is why they married who they married.

The likes of Buster and your dad, they were pretty attractive people. And the likes of your mother and Mugs were most likely good-
looking chicks and individuals in their day. Maybe they didn't like
getting tied up with some guy who was arranged for them. They
were rebels in their own way, they went with who they wanted to.
It's better to go out with a fast-talking half-Chinaman who's working in a restaurant and who's got a good line of bullshit.

But my mother, she hasn't got any wildness in her.

How come she went with your dad?

I don't know. Maybe she was a bit unruly back then. But then
your mom. Well, the stories I heard about her, sneaking out, at a
young age, running around, smoking.

Which was an unforgivable sin, smoking. And Granny Wah was
pretty strict, too.

My mom tells the story about your mom being one of the first
girls in Swift Current to smoke.

I wouldn't doubt it a bit. She's a pretty headstrong person. But
like you say, the very same thing, why would Mugs end up with
Buster and your mother end up with Fred? These guys here were
hard-working guys in the restaurant. It's not as if they were your
typical high school kids.

Well now, they must have had something to do with high school.
I know my dad went to school when he got back from China, had to
go to night school or something. And don't forget, Swift Current
was a small town in those days—everyone knew everybody. So they
had the chance to date. Lil and Andy were definitely horsing around

because they would take my mom and dad in the rumble seat in whatever car Andy could borrow and they would go out to Maple Creek to basketball games.

What I understand is that your dad was very much in love, it was a courtship, and he wanted to sweep your mother right off her feet.

Yeah, they were very much in love. But those guys were spiffy, too.

Very shiny shoes.

So I think they were probably—well you can imagine Swift Current being like a farmer/working class town. Well Buster, and my dad, and your dad, Andy, a traveling salesman, probably pretty spiffy too—that those guys were seen as having some money and being big spenders.

Yeah, they had bucks that everybody didn't have. They had cash in their pockets, whether it was from tips or wages, They didn't have to worry about food, they could eat in the restaurant.

A rather risqué element in Swift Current in the thirties, these Chinese kids with a little change in their pockets.

Which would be very appealing for young girls.

But not very appealing to their parents.

No, that's right. The Aikens were unhappy and the Ericksons were unhappy. But the end results, except for the Aikens and the Ericksons in Swift Current, as we see every family reunion, have been well worth it.

Yeah, we've been pretty lucky.

*T*HE EARLY MORNING RUSH
IS OVER BY 7:30

and he can grab a bite to eat. This morning he gets some toast, a few pieces of bacon, a cup of coffee, and a *Nelson Daily News* and sits on the corner stool next to the percolator so he can watch the till while Donna waits on the customers and cleans up.

Before turning to the sports pages Fred quickly checks the front page headlines. He squints and concentrates when he reads. Silently he articulates the news to himself:

More snow today, but only down to five below tonight. If it warms up a bit we'll be really busy tomorrow, everybody in town shopping. Just three shopping days until Christmas. The whole weekend'll be busy, that'll be good.

Look at this, the New Star's put in a Christmas ad. I better call Art Gibbon and get one in for the Diamond for Christmas Eve. New Year's too, probably.

Hey, good, here's that stuff about the special classes for the Chinese kids:

> Fifteen new Canadians from China desiring to become better citizens have embarked on courses to better learn our language, geography and history. The fifteen new Nelson residents range in age from seventeen to twenty-one. They will attend a special class at the Central School. A teacher, Miss K. Porter, has been provided and classes will commence January 3, 1952.

Sure a lot of kids coming over now they're letting them in. They'll be o.k. Be nice to have some more Chinese around to talk to.

Gee, that Boxing Day hockey game with Spokane doesn't start

until three. There'll probably be a big crowd in here for supper after the game. I better put on another waitress in case.

He doesn't quite make it to last night's curling scores before he has to jump up to make change at the till. Then he tosses down the last few bits of bacon and slurps his coffee on his way back to the kitchen.

This day's gonna be a real runner, he thinks to himself.

*M*Y FATHER NEVER SCREAMS.
WHEN HE GETS MAD

at me or my brothers his voice is angry with a kind of whispered tightness, a lot of force but it isn't loud and explosive.

When I do acid in the sixties, one of the horrifying visions I have during what turns into a Tibetan Book of the Dead bad trip is of a baby's mouth howling so wide open you can see down its throat.

Christ, the sound of fury. Your own. Don't pull the cord until you're all alone.

*U*NTIL MARY MCNUTTER
CALLS ME A CHINK I'M

not one. That's in elementary school. Later, I don't have to be because I don't look like one. But just then, I'm stunned. I've never thought about it. After that I start to listen, and watch. Some people are different. You can see it. Or hear it.

The old Chinamen have always been friends of my dad's. They give us kids candy. I go fishing down by the boat-houses with one of them. He's a nice man, shiny brown knuckles, baits my hook, shows me how to catch mudsuckers, shows me how to row a boat. We're walking back up the hill with our catch of suckers and some kids start chinky, chinky Chinaman and I figure I'd better not be caught with him anymore.

I become as white as I can, which, considering I'm mostly Scandinavian, is pretty easy for me. Not for my dad and some of my cousins though. They're stuck, I think, with how they look. I only have the name to contend with. And I not only hear my friends put down the Chinks (and the Japs, and the Wops, and the Spiks, and the Douks) but comic books and movies confirm that the Chinese are yellow (meaning cowardly), not-to-be trusted, heathens, devils, slant-eyed, dirty, and talk incomprehensible gobblydee-gook. Thus: gook n. *Slang.* 1. A dirty, sludgy, or slimy substance. 2. An Oriental. An offensive term used derogatorily. Even now a half-Ukrainian-half-Japanese daughter of a friend of mine calls anyone, white or not, who doesn't fit, a Geek. Even her father, who, we all know, is really a Nip.

Sticks and stones might break my bones, but names will never hurt me.

$\mathcal{W}$HENEVER I GO TO HIM,

STRAIGHT, THERE'S NEVER

any problem.

Like the time I decide I need a good fountain pen, something glitzy and adult, but when I ask my mom she says forget it, they're too expensive, you don't need something like that. So I go down to see my dad at the cafe later that day and tell him I need a good fountain pen, it'll help me do better work at school. There's a good one over at Benwell's Stationery for four dollars and twenty cents. He says o.k. if you think it'll help your school work. Of course Mom tears a strip off of me when she finds out.

Or, like the night I let my dad know I've started smoking. My dad smokes and when I get hooked I don't say anything to him. I'm pretty sure he knows but he never says anything. Still, it's not something I let on to around home. I'm studying for my finals down in my basement room, I'm nervous and I want a cigarette. I decide this is it, I'll ask him. So I go upstairs and say Hey Dad I really need a smoke, is it alright with you if I smoke in the house? He says sure, that's o.k. Then I ask can I bum one of yours? He smiles a little and passes me his pack of Players Mild from out of his shirt pocket, a sky-blue package and the word *Hero* written on the sailor's cap.

past and to the right of the chopping block. The handle's a hefty snap-lock galvanized device because this door's large, insulated, and heavy too. Friday mornings the fresh milk's delivered in ten-gallon cans; be careful to skim the fresh cream off the top with a slow and steady ladle. This is the cream for the coffee and breakfast cereals, almost sweet.

A good-sized walk-in cooler, ten by ten, with shelves lining three walls for meats, cheeses, pastries, sauces, salad makings, Jell-Os, butter patties, the dark and the cool. Where Seto puts the extra Boston cream pies and, oh sweet tooth treasure, that large whipping cream syringe; a heavy cloth cone fitted with an icing nipple at one end. There's a smaller one up at the soda fountain too, for sundaes and hot chocolate, but this one, when I run into the cooler, alone, so easy and quick to squeeze a gob onto a finger and lick it off. This is the biggest and heaviest door in the cafe. When I slam it shut with its great metallic clank, all those Chinese guys in the kitchen hear my hard work underlined and me going past fast, their critical gazes silenced by my busy busy blaze.

H

E NEVER GETS BLUE.
HE'LL GET RED WHEN

he drinks, which is seldom. I never see him get red from embarrassment. When he's mad he'll get a black look about him. Even blacker because he has a dark complexion and black hair anyway. According to the kids at school, he's supposed to be yellow, but I don't see it.

Way back somewhere, Swift Current or Trail, I get hold of some wooden matches, out on a porch, play around with them, light a few, until my mother catches me and says just wait until your father gets home, he comes home from work, and I get a real spanking, the spanking of my life my mother says, still says.

Or, a sunny winter Sunday in East Trail about 1946, a bunch of us are sleigh-riding and a bus, trying to make it up the hill through all the kids, honks its horn, and I turn into a smart-aleck and yell out something jerky like get that stupid bus outa the way, so then the bus driver gets out of the bus and all us kids freeze and he comes over to confront my yappiness. Stupidly I give him my name and he says he knows who my dad is and he's going to tell him what I've done. When I get home my mom warns me that I'm in real hot water and just wait'll your dad gets home. The next couple of hours are pretty bad. Finally he comes in and boy does he shake me up. I not only get a spanking but I get a good talking to about how I can't fool around out there when my father's a business man, a Chinese business man, and I'd better not talk back like I did today, to anyone, particularly when they're white, because it all comes down on him, my father, and our family has to be careful in this town it's a small town and don't ever think you're so smart if you think that hurts wait until you try horsing around like this again and I'll give you a good reason to cry. He says the bus driver went to the police so I'd better get ready to go to jail. I have to confess and apologize to the police chief on the phone.

He gets bugged with me, I suppose, for good reason, but that's usually just parents and kids and part of growing up. Daily stuff.

But when he gets really mad, the colour of that is black and blue.

Looks like it's going to snow all day.

No point in doing the sidewalk yet.

Fred's mornings are always full of dialogue. When he isn't yakking with a customer he talks to himself in a kind of play-by-play commentary.

Look at that. Those kids eating doughnuts for breakfast. She should know better than to just give them money for breakfast. Why doesn't she come in here with them, she doesn't have to be at work yet. Crazy family. I'd never let that happen to my kids.

Gotta call Koehle to come and fix that cooler for the soda fountain. He probably won't come today though because they play the Smokies in Trail tonight.

Hi there Bob, what're you gonna have this morning?

Shit, those lazy guys on night shift again, didn't fill the ketchup last night.

Look at old Gilchrist, shoveling his own sidewalk. Why doesn't he leave it for the hired help?

Jeezus christ, here comes Ed Bentall. He looks like hell. Been out all night again, gambling upstairs at the Percolator Club. I bet he lost a bundle. Just before Christmas too.

Hiya Ed, wanna coffee?

Yeah, and get me a pack of Export 'A' Freddy.

Comin' right up. Here ya go. Alley oop!

THE COFFEE URN'S A BIG
STAINLESS DOUBLE WITH

glass tubes down the front so you can see the level of the coffee. The whole counter in fact is shiny stainless and easy to wipe up. Whoever opens up in the morning, usually my dad or his partner Shu the cook, turns on the urn and lights the stove in the kitchen, both gas. Turning on the urn also means opening the water valves to fill each urn. When the water gets hot enough you pour it over about ten cups of ground, some egg shells and a little salt, all held in a cloth sack hanging inside of the urn and fixed in place by a large metal hoop.

The urn is always steaming away and it's a tough job to lift out the scalding sacks of ground coffee and take them to the kitchen to rinse them out for re-use.

Under the urn are shelves for cups and teapots and on the counter is a big tin of Malkin's cocoa powder (one large tablespoon of cocoa mixed into a paste with canned cream and stirred in hot water).

This is the centre of the cafe, the place to yak it up with the other waiters and waitresses, to kid around, complain about the bad tippers, to change shifts, to unload an armful of dirty dishes into a tub, and, often, more than once, to get a wink, a pinch, and a smile from Donna Mori. Caffeine junction's always buzzing.

Spring, Stanley Cup playoffs, you away and your

grades arrive from university. I can't wait to find out how you've done and don't open them, because you asked us not to, but I hold the envelope up to the sunlight and can see some Fs. Jeezus F. Christ I'm mad. I get so worked up about it I phone one of your profs and he tells me that you haven't even attended his classes for the past couple of months. Wah! I hit the roof. Lucky for you, maybe lucky for me too, that you won't be back for a few weeks, so I have a chance to simmer down. I'm still pretty ticked off at you by the time you get home.

But I love you. It all works out. You and I have done alright, our genealogical trajectories compounded or diluted enough into the white middle class to put us over the blue line; I can't stay mad at you forever. I've learned family has its own irrelevant anticipations, though my love for you is as solid as the Civic Centre ice you fell on during the figure skating club show, my own heart twanging in tandem to your embarrassment. What is that ratio of anger and sympathy that hovers around the household arena and needs to be flooded so often? We need to Zamboni our love smooth until it shines, around and around, past the nets, down the centre, right out of the rink.

I COMPLAIN TO MY MOM
ONE NIGHT THAT

I deserve a raise. Now, after working in the cafe for a couple of years, now that I know the ropes, I think I should get more than twenty-five cents an hour. Thirty-five, perhaps. I'm too scared to ask him, so I try to get her to take my side.

I think I got the raise; it brought my weekly paycheck up to about two eighty-five, plus tips, maybe five bucks. But he never mentioned it to me. I certainly never asked him for it face-to-face.

THE PASTRY COOK IN THE DIAMOND IS ONE

of the four partners. All Seto does is the desserts; pies, butter tarts, doughnuts, even the Christmas cakes. We think he's pretty lazy but we also think he's one of the best. He has his butterhorns come out fresh for the morning coffee break and there are seldom any left by the afternoon. He's always one Boston cream pie ahead in the kitchen cooler. His coconut and banana cream pies are perfection, but his lemon meringue disappears almost before it's in the display case. I like his butter tarts a lot; they and maybe a few jelly doughnuts are the only things ever left over and brought home by my dad.

For Midsummer Bonspiel Seto always features a strawberry shortcake; curlers from The Pas and Brooks, Alberta, return summer after summer, they claim, for a piece of Seto's strawberry shortcake. Miss Freeman from Sterling Home Furniture phones just before lunch asking us to hold a piece for her because she knows she'll be late.

His sugar doughnuts are legendary throughout the Kootenays. They come out fresh about two thirty every afternoon and are pretty hard to resist when warm. One of my innovations as the soda jerk is the doughnut sundae. Big, puffy sugar doughnut with a scoop of vanilla ice cream in the centre topped with either marshmallow or strawberry, a floret of whipped cream and chopped peanuts. Only myself and a few of my friends ever have Seto's doughnuts this way. My dad says it looks awful.

Seto rolls his dough out in a small room next to the office. It's Seto's pantry and it doesn't have a door. No one else has any reason to go in there anyway. It's full of flour and sugar and a great big dough beater. He gets his doughnuts rising on big trays and then deep fries them over on the main cookstove. Usually he makes his pies out at the table in the main kitchen so he can talk at the cooks and the dishwasher. Most of the time, though, he just stands around smoking; I've never seen him move fast, like everyone else who works here. Maybe he put more money in than the other partners so he doesn't have to work as hard. He's usually gone by four or five in the afternoon.

I BUST MY ASS TO GIVE THOSE KIDS

everything they need but they always want more!

My dad's arguing with my mother in the hall just outside my bedroom. He's on his way to work and they're talking about the raise I asked for the night before.

He's lucky to get what he gets, he says to her. How the hell does he think he's worth so much? Always only thinking of himself. He takes time off whenever he's got something else to do, he's always leaving early, and now he thinks I don't pay him enough. I'm doing him a favour to let him work in the cafe. He eats more than he's worth anyway. I always let him off whenever he wants to go to hockey or basketball trips. He sleeps in on Sundays. What more does he want? He better pull his socks up 'cause when he gets out on his own no one's gonna be there to look after him and he'll find out things aren't so easy. He should work for nothing, the lazy bugger. You tell him that if he doesn't like what I pay him then he should get another job. Christ, this kid better smarten up in a hurry or I'll give him a good swift one he won't forget!

*I*T COULD BE AS IRRELEVANT
AS POUTING EACH

time the Socreds win and the NDP don't. For my father and many of
his Chinese friends from the Canton region it is Chiang Kai-shek
and the communists.

Down on Lake Street the Chinese Nationalist League has a large
portrait of Chiang in the main room. The only reason I can ever
figure out for this house-slash-political organization is to hold
Chinese banquets. And there are plenty of them, and lots of kids and
free Coke and great food. The men play mah-jong upstairs and
smoke and talk a lot; absence of Chinese women.

Also later, I realize how important that place, the Nationalist
League, is for these people. Their only real polis is what is happen-
ing in China. With Mao's victory in 1949 these Chinese Nationalists
in Nelson are the only hope for some of the refugees from that civil
war.

But no wonder my grandfather, my father, and their kin continue
to look back at China. Canada couldn't be an investment for them.
The 1923 Chinese Act of Exclusion isn't repealed until 1947. Even
though my dad was born in Medicine Hat, he wasn't allowed to vote
until 1948. Nor are any of the other *orientals* in Canada.

When I ask my father about the small portrait of Chiang at the
top of the stairs in our house, he says that guy is a general in China.
He fights the communists. King George is the portrait I see in some
of my friends' houses. At first I think Chiang means king. But we
don't sing "God save Chiang" at school; we sing to a portrait outside
the principal's office, to a doll-like gracious king with porcelain skin
and boy-scout-grey eyes who is the *real* king of the world.

ON THE EDGE OF CENTRE.
JUST OFF MAIN.

Chinatown. The cafes, yes, but further back, almost hidden, the ubiquitous Chinese store—an unmoving stratus of smoke, dusky and quiet, clock ticking. Dark brown wood paneling, some porcelain planters on the windowsill, maybe some goldfish. Goldfish for Gold Mountain men. Not so far, then, from the red carp of their childhood ponds. Brown skin stringy salt-and-pepper beard polished bent knuckles and at least one super-long fingernail for picking. Alone and on the edge of their world, far from the centre, no women, no family. This kind of edge in race we only half suspect as edge. A gap, really. Hollow.

I wander to it, tagging along with my father or with a cousin, sent there to get a jar of some strange herb or balm from an old man who forces salted candies on us or digs for a piece of licorice dirtied with grains of tobacco from his pocket, the background of old men's voices sure and argumentative within this grotto. Dominoes clacking. This store, part of a geography, mysterious to most, a migrant haven edge of outpost, of gossip, bavardage, foreign tenacity. But always in itself, on the edge of some great fold.

In a room at the back of the Chinese store, or above, like a room fifteen feet over the street din in Vancouver Chinatown, you can hear, amplified through the window, the click-clacking of mah-jong pieces being shuffled over the table tops. The voices from up there or behind the curtain are hot-tempered, powerful, challenging, aggressive, bickering, accusatory, demeaning, bravado, superstitious, bluffing, gossipy, serious, goading, letting off steam, ticked off, fed up, hot under the collar, hungry for company, hungry for language, hungry for luck, edgy.

DEEP FRIED WHOLE ROCK COD IS A SPECIAL

dish. It's a little hard to get sometimes on the prairies, so they often substitute pickerel, acceptable though a little less fleshy. But at a Chinatown fish market in Vancouver I can pick up half a dozen rock or ling weighing in at about thirty pounds. They're quite fresh so, rather than freeze them, I decide to keep them in ice for the couple of days it'll take to get up to Windermere for the family reunion.

On the day of the banquet we set up Ray's big propane cooker outside the kitchen door of the community hall. We're going to deep fry these fish in a huge wok. Uncle Andy wears heavy leather work gloves while he scales the fish; these fish have scales sharp enough to cut right through a finger. Uncle Roy scores each fish down both sides before he deep fries it for about five minutes. He and my brother Ernie lift each fish out of the oil onto a platter using a cedar shake in each hand. The fish are kept warm in an oven.

Aunty Ethel has pre-cooked a large pot of sauce that is ladled over the fish just before serving. Her sauce is a basic sweet-and-pungent tomato sauce made with canned tomatoes, a couple of tablespoons each of sugar, soy sauce and vinegar, ginger, some chopped celery and green onions, a few red and green peppers, with cornstarch added to thicken.

The skin is crisp and, with chopsticks, chunks of white flesh come away from the bones easily until all that's left is a head and skeleton. I don't see anyone in our family now who goes for the eyes like Grampa used to.

THE COOK'S ANGER, SCOWLY.
BACK BEHIND SOME UNCLE

merchant son's false papers that got him into this land of hope. A wife caught behind the lines after the Japanese took over Guangzhou. The hassle to get her and his son over here even after the Chinese Exclusion Act's repealed in 1947. A life with nothing but grease, smoke, and sweat over a hot stove and then the lonely walk home.

Or the dishwasher's gloom as he lifts a basket of cutlery from under the scalding hot tap and empties it clanging onto the large stainless-steel draining board, no wife, no children, an entire life of jobs in back rooms and kitchens.

Even Pong the old gambler, the silent partner of the cafe, when he comes into the kitchen every morning about ten-thirty for his rice and soup, sits there and curses in Chinese while he sips a glass of whiskey and tea and smokes a cigarette, berating the others with what sounds like I told you so you stupid dog bastards. Look at me; I'm willing to take some chances!

All of them in the kitchen, grumpy and fractious.

At what?

When I ask my dad he just says They're like that. They've always been like that!

Him then? Me, too?

𝒯HE STOVE AT THE
DIAMOND IS A BIG

gas model, twelve feet long. Most of its surface is grill, though there are some gas burners for quick boiling at one end. The pots are scattered over the surface like curling rocks, at various places for different temperatures. The grill's kept shiny clean with a folded sack and spatulas that scrape the used oil into a trough along the front that collects it into a big can at one end. A bank of ovens under the grill provides the roasts and keeps a few things warm.

Across from the stove and between the cooks and the waiters is the steam counter. That's where the roasts, the gravy, and the vegetables are kept and where the cook puts the orders together. We also dish up the soup du jour there.

To the right of the steam counter is the sandwich counter. That's also where we get the two slices of bread served with every meal or where we pop in the toast as we place an order of two soft-under-glass, side a bacon.

The cook, Shu, who runs the kitchen, is also one of my dad's partners. He works as hard as my dad or even harder. It's bloody hot over that stove and Shu is a large, fairly plump man. He's never without a cigarette dangling from his lips and if any ashes fall into a plate of food he'll take the corner of a mop-up towel around his thumb and just wipe them off. Same deft move for any gravy dripping off the edge of the plate.

Shu has a scornful countenance, and his big puffy eyes don't help. He'll curse at all of us, particularly when we leave an order sitting too long. Except for older waitresses like Mrs. Morrison; he's pretty civil to her and I don't blame him, since she's about as big as he is and can handily take on any high muckamuck who gives her trouble.

Mary Morrison, in fact, will even walk around to the other side of the big serving counter to the stove and cook her own eggs. I must have witnessed the first time she did this because Shu couldn't believe it. He just stood aside with his hand on his hip while she flipped her eggs on the grill and said That's how I like 'em, stiff as a preacher's tongue but soft in the middle.

*S*ALESMEN START COMING INTO THE
KITCHEN AROUND EIGHT.

Shu scolds most of them while he's flipping, scraping, and stirring at the stove.

Hey, ya know that box of Brussels sprouts they brought up yesterday? Half of 'em are rotten, no good. Whatdya think I'm supposed to do with them? You better get me some good ones by Monday or that'll ruin our Christmas menu.

Shu keeps most of his ordering in his head and he doesn't miss a thing. Then Fred usually comes in and hits the guy backside.

Jezus christ, Wilson, look at this, he says, getting an invoice from the office. You told me these hams would be forty-nine a pound and they're charging us fifty-five. What're ya trying to do, put us out of business?

One of the city cops stands there looking on from the back kitchen door. He's just stopped in for a free coffee and doughnut and Shu talks to him about the bad weather and all the car accidents.

Wilson flips open his order book and stands ready: Hey Freddy, Shu, anything you need last minute to be delivered Monday? You got enough coffee? Any paper products? Don't forget we won't be delivering now until next Thursday.

Shu laughs and says bring us one of these, pointing to a bare-breasted pin-up calendar.

Fred invites Wilson into the office so he can spike his coffee, a ritual he loves at this time of year. He can't drink himself but he gets a great kick out of offering it to everyone else.

There are ten cafes in town. By the time Wilson gets back to Malkin's for the Christmas office party (if he does) he'll be pretty pickled.

*a*ND YOU, OLD, MUMBLING TO
YOURSELF SWEDISH GRAMPA,

what madnesses of northern Europe in 1922 drove you across an ocean to Saskatchewan? Uprooted, lost or new? What are you doing up there, silent on a wooden height in the sun and wind, nailing grain elevator after grain elevator. What sour images immigrated with you to that horizon, that languagelessness? His answer full of angst and sadness.

No. They weren't sour. Up here nailing nailing, the pictures of Uppsala and Vastmanland, my father cutting cordwood in the forest, the old city, streets and friends, this is erased slowly and softly, empty prairie wind whipped into the corners of my eyes, my mind, memory hammered into, day after day on the scaffold. But to hell with it, it's work.

This sky is the world now.

I know no one except for a few others on this job. On Saturday we'll have a few beers, relax a bit. Not like back home. Too much church.

After the war, lots of work. My brother got a good job in Göteborg, in the shipyards. He suggested we move there, he could get me on easily he said. But really, it was the same old thing. I wanted something different.

This sky is different: larger, bluer, farther. Maybe it will be different here. Maybe I will be different.

Smell this pine we're working with, still wet and bleeding pitch, turpentine. They say all our wood here comes from the mountains to the west. I believe it. You can smell that hot summer wind blowing pine bite through the forests anywhere, everywhere, over this prairie, over this ocean.

THE DOORWAY TO THE BASEMENT IS TO THE

left of Seto's pantry shelves. Once in awhile I see the old-man dish-washer appear from the darkness of that doorway with a pail of peeled spuds. One day my dad takes me down there to show me how to shut off the hookups for the soda water. The descent does not beckon; it is dimly lit. My dad moves down the steps with a raised arm, fishing for the hanging pull-strings to the few light bulbs. The basement smells of cat piss; the mousers live down here.

Under a single light bulb, sitting on a stool between a sack of potatoes and some galvanized buckets full of water, is a young Chinese kid, about my age. He looks up and smiles. My dad says a few words to him in Chinese and he laughs back and then goes on peeling. I've never seen him before. When I ask, my dad tells me that's Wing Bo, a nephew of the dishwasher. He came over from China a little while ago. Can't speak English yet.

A couple of days later I have to go to the basement for some more paper napkins and I say hi to Wing Bo as I walk past. His eyes light up and he starts to say something in Chinese. I just say sorry I can only speak English. He looks lonely. When he realizes we're not going to be able to talk he just holds up a cleanly peeled spud and laughs. I tell him what a great job he's doing by sticking my thumb in the air. We both sputter meaningless phrases and get on with our work.

I try to get down to the basement more often and kid around a bit with Wing Bo and in a couple of weeks we're arm twisting. Eventually he learns a little English and a couple of years later he's out front cleaning tables.

I think he went to Vancouver. Whenever I'm in Chinatown I keep an eye out for his welcoming face. He was a good guy, a happy paper son.

*T*HE CAFE ITSELF IS A LONG, NARROW ROOM
with two horseshoe counters and the soda fountain up front, and
then three rows of booths. The two outside rows along the walls,
about a dozen booths, can seat six tightly, which is how the kids
from school jam into them. There's another row of smaller booths
down the middle that only seat two apiece. At the back, under a
large framed Chinese dragon embroidered on white silk and breathing fire, is a large circular booth that can seat about ten, fifteen if you
use chairs.

Frequently the large booth is used for short coffee-break meet-
ings of one sort or another amongst some of the Baker Street nickel
millionaires. It's usually pretty lively around that booth at 10:30 in
the morning, full of a bunch of businessmen in suits and my dad
timbering them for their coffee.

Timber's a coin game. You put your hand in your pocket and take
out from zero to three coins and put your clenched fist into the circle of other clenched fists. Everyone tries to guess the total number
of coins. My dad always wins more than he loses and he puts his
winnings in a big plastic piggy bank at home every night. He gives
that piggy bank to me for Christmas the first year I go to university.

The booths have only semi-high backs, so it's easy to see whoever
is in the cafe. They're upholstered in orange and green Naugahyde
and there's a chrome coat pole at the end of each seat. The most
modern-looking thing about the restaurant is that these booths are
built on a slight diagonal, diamond-shaped, to make better use of the
narrowness of the room. I don't know if it's the shape of the tables
that gave the Diamond its name or vice versa. Whatever, the place is
considered the most modern and up-to-date of the half-dozen
Chinese cafes in town.

Between the last booth and the kitchen are the bathrooms and the waitresses' change room. There's also a little sink right behind that last booth so if you come out of the kitchen and see a customer come in you can pick up a glass of water and a menu and get to them as soon as they sit down. My dad insists that a good waiter always brings a glass of water the very first thing.

That back booth is also where the waitresses have their meals and where my dad will sometimes sit down with his 11:30 lunch of some Chinese dish the cook has produced for the Chinese workers. When we're on shift we're allowed to eat the specials and help ourselves to pastries within reason. Once I ordered something outrageous like a porterhouse steak and the cook got really mad at me. In fact, the few Chinese words I know are the ones I hear in the kitchen when the cooks swear at me.

Thloong you!

You mucka high!

WHAT'S ALREADY IN THE GROUND, ROOTS OF ANOTHER

body, carpel leaf and tunnel, fragment of stone, simple weight of saviour, fossil, marrow, bone, translation of immediate skin map, lime and spine, pigment and pore, preamble to yet another quiet almost cloudhead thunder building, saying get to the end, compass pointing, magnetic declination included, Chinese ink strokes too, a little purple and green from the lottery sheets, eye wanders into the middle of whose book, whose gutter, a bit of fearful symmetry, swaying of the transit plumb bob, hand across mind's eye, intimate life lines scanned, sudden word for number, sudden rose destroyed, skipping, rope, a little oriented anchor mediation, a taken token, yak-yak din of the Hermes draught caught from across the room, rattling of the mantic dice, the padded paws of adverbs, *punctum* of metaphor camouflaged into the leaves of the page, the stars of text as a cloudless sky, whisper of tires down the distant freeway, ciped tableaus of voyage forgetting, the raiments of message or the caprice of house grammar, smell the meltdown, remember the pear tree, are the membranes paper thin, are the layers of dream time disappearing, these are the details under foot, this is the soil the clay the mud, this is the dirt of dying.

I CAN ALWAYS TELL, WHEN
OUR FAMILY WALKS

into a Chinese restaurant where my dad isn't known (like Vancouver), that the Chinese there eyeball him with a little contempt. First off they're usually surprised when he speaks to them in Cantonese. And when they scan the rest of us you can sense they're a little uneasy and curious about why his family's white.

My dad's pretty easygoing in such familiar territory and pretty soon they're exchanging all sorts of information about mutual acquaintances, who's working where, who's going back to China to get a wife, how's business, and so forth. After the meal, Dad goes into the kitchen to talk with the cooks. And the waiters bring us kids something special, like lichee nuts or ginger candy. By the end of the meal, they refuse to let him pay the bill, insisting that it's on the house.

But I can tell.

*a*ROUND QUARTER TO TEN THE
MORNING COFFEE RUSH

starts. The first ones in are the eager seconds-in-command from
Woolworth's and Eaton's across the street. They started work at
eight and this is their first break for a cigarette and coffee. They're
quick, no more than fifteen minutes. They might have a butterhorn
or sugar doughnut but usually they just have time for a smoke. They
gulp their coffee and twist and turn on the rotary stools at the
counter as they compare jobs and potential seasonal parties.

The main morning action in the cafe, however, is in the large oval
booth at the back with the nickel millionaires. Some mornings there
might be eight, ten of the high muckamuck store owners and insur-
ance salesmen pow-wowing town power. They complain about the
mayor and the highways department, they compare curling scores,
and they talk business and service club and hockey and the high cost
of freight—and Fred plays timber with them.

They start out betting just for coffee but no one can stand to lose
so the stakes go up. He taunts them with jokes about their luck, he
loves it. Digging his right hand into his change pocket he'll rattle the
coins and challenge the boys to another round, o.k. Phillips, c'mon,
don't be such a cheapskate, I'll give you a chance to get your money
back, two bits, put up or shut up. They can't resist, everybody shoves
a hand into a pocket and comes out with clenched fist slapping on
the table and screened glances deke one another's eyes. Each hand
can hold from zero to three coins and each player guesses at the total.
Around the table they go, getting their digs in at one another's bluffing tactics until the last man calls out his number and snaps open his
hand to reveal zero one two or three coins, they total the coins
around the table and the closest hunch wins.

He loves this friendly back-booth horsing around. It's good for business and these customers like it. He also wins more than he loses. Every night he empties his pocket of coins into a large plastic piggy bank so that by Christmas he can buy something special for the house or for Connie.

So, there, one Christmas morning spread out on the living room floor beside the tree and wrapping and ribbon debris all the nickels quarters dimes pennies and fifty-cent pieces arranged into piles to be counted and rolled into those special coin sheets you get from the bank, money money money spangled with his proud gambling smile and wink to us kids that he could do that, bluff each day past those white guys and always have jingle jangle high jinks deep into his right pocket for his family and his own head to hold up to the face of whatever fortune chance luck can be held there in the close darkness of the right-hand palm lined with looking out for. Then wow, for this Christmas I'm the winner, he gives me the bank, three hundred and twenty-six dollars and ninety-two cents, he says pretty good, eh, that's for university, your timber scholarship Freddy. Easy games get serious.

*A*NOTHER CHIP ON MY SHOULDER
IS THE APPROPRIATION

of the immigrant identity. I see it all over the place. Even one of the country's best-known writers has said We are all immigrants to this place even if we were born here. Can't these people from *central* leave anything to itself? Why deny the immigrant his or her real world? Why be in such a rush to dilute? Those of us who have already been genetically diluted need our own space to figure it out. I don't want to be inducted into someone else's story, or project. Particularly one that would reduce and usurp my family's residue of ghost values to another status quo. Sorry, but I'm just not interested in this collective enterprise erected from the sacrosanct great railway imagination dedicated to harvesting a dominant white cultural landscape. There's a whole forest of us out here who don't like clear-cut, suspect the mechanical purity of righteous, clear, shining, Homelite Americas, chainsaws whining, just across the valley.

No way I'll let these chips fall where they may.

*T*HE DISHWASHER IS A THIN, OLD
MAN WHOSE ONLY

jobs are to wash dishes and peel potatoes. He works from eight in the morning to seven at night. I never hear him say a word—he moves his eyes instead of his lips.

Carry in an armload of dirty dishes and while yelling out a new order to the cook—grilled cheese on brown, ham an', Denver san'!—dump them into a large stainless steel sorting trough, throwing the cutlery into a wooden bucket. If it's rush hour everything's just left for the dishwasher to sort through, but if it's slack we're supposed to scrape the scraps into the slop hole. The only Chinese farmer in the Koots, Charlie Bing, comes in a couple of times a week to get the slop for his pigs.

The dishwasher sprays off the plates in the trough with a hose and then moves them into large sinks along the wall where he'll wash and rinse.

When he isn't cleaning dishes he leans over a bucket peeling potatoes or carrots—silent (where on earth?)—the others jabbering, but never to him.

Sometimes I'm in the kitchen doing a bunch of different things and he just sits there, on his Coke box, smoking a cigarette and keeps his eyes on me the whole time. Tracks. No name. Circum the person.

EVEN THEIR DARK EYES.
A KIND OF AFTERBIRTH

of noise in finality and shock at the big cooler door in the kitchen and the cook's faces impetuous and scowly when the latch clunks shut. A simple door shutting in the running rhythm and rush of a cafe kitchen, but with the insulated mass of a concussive jolt, of a sonar synapse, for these old brown men at least, along some other wire of their lives. The discharge of a door, electric in the nodes of memory. Trauma and dreams. Metal locks nick the margin of noise and surface notates their distances, kindles the dark eyes into a long sea water gaze *Pacifica* dazed from absence. Abstinence. The sound of grass beyond the brass. Piggy bank reverence for copper coins. Sudden acrid throat and the bicameral tumblers sparked shockwave blip simple breathing of the magnetic dip. The silk intelligence of memory stumbling for the lost endogene. Undreamed-of switching device substrate in the echo. Lake of idling engines. Sieve and colander for the yelping of dogs. Cow-tow the big doors bark. Bow wow!

THE SAFE IS IN THE OFFICE AND THE

office is between the pastry room and the cooler, all three rooms at the far end of the kitchen, at the very back of the cafe, along the alley. The small office window has metal bars. My dad usually goes back at night to work on the books. And if we don't have rice at home for supper, he'll always go back for that. But he'll work in the office doing the day's tabs, close the till down at ten o'clock, and then put everything away in the safe, a large heavy metal box on wheels with a scratched-up colourful decal of a mountain landscape on its door. I've only seen inside it once and was disappointed that, instead of neat stacks of rubber-banded greenbacks, all I could see were bundles of paper and a few cigar boxes.

Before they owned a safe he'd have to take the cash home and put it in his top dresser drawer until he could get it to the bank the next day. And when he was in the Elite in Trail, before we had a car, he'd have to walk home late at night with the cash in a bag and a pistol in his pocket.

*I*N OUR FAMILY WE CALL IT GIM JIM

but when you order it in a cafe you'll have more success calling it gum jum. My brother Donnie makes this dish of lily buds with steamed chicken and its sweet musky taste is singular and memorable.

The dried, elongated lily buds, about two to three inches long, are a pale gold colour, fragile and lightweight until they have been soaked for close to an hour in warm water. Rinse, cut off their ends, and then tie each one in a half knot. While the gim jim is soaking, chop up a chicken with a cleaver, bones and all, into one-and-a-half-to two-inch chunks. Sliver some bamboo shoots, water chestnuts, and ginger root into a bowl of two tablespoons of soy sauce, a shot of whiskey, pinches of salt and sugar, and a few drops of sesame oil. Blend all the ingredients together in a heat-proof bowl, set the bowl in a large pot or wok, and surround the bowl to about two-thirds of its height with boiling water. Cover the pot and steam for about fifteen minutes.

Gim jim, yum yum.

CHINESE HEAD TAX PAID OUT
LAND GRANTS TO

European settlers of the prairie marsh pre-1923 fingered for slant-eyed yellowed family vista visa home boat railway crossed and exed out John A.'s apple for dirty Chinks re strict and ex clude peril from the horde head count done for now since stack blew the gasket but never bone-brown Grampa Wah'd white Canada's xeno-heat for long shimmered their open portals union jacked adapt miscegenated legislated fish heads for the dog world under one mat per month of rice let them peddle gimcracks stewed opiate moon-eyed flipped herbs beyond the Long March and the writing on the Great Wall we want pigtails and gold dust and the celestial bones returned assets attest threat. This certifies that under the provisions of the Chinese Immigration Act <u>Charley Chim Chong Say Wong Liu Chung</u> a native of <u>The Peach Garden</u> in the <u>Kingdom of Laundry</u> of the age <u>ancient</u> years and whose title official rank profession or occupation is that of a <u>rented muscle</u> who arrived or landed at <u>Gold Mountain</u> on the <u>auspicious</u> day of <u>the Yellow Pages</u> 190_ <u>1858, 1885, 1903, 1923, 1947</u> Vide statement and declaration form No. <u>one son</u> has <u>(never will be)</u> paid the fee or duty imposed upon Chinese Immigrants on their arrival in Canada <u>NOT, no Chinky way</u> being exempt from such payment under the terms of the said Act, and has been registered at <u>Craigellachie and Chinaman's Peak</u> under the No. <u>eight spot</u> in the day month and year hereunto affixed[†] controlled jumped Onderdonked leveled pooled under the fifty-five-foot deep

---

[†] Text for Head Tax Certificate and B. C. Sugar Refinery ad taken from *East Meets West*, ed. by Francis Hardwick (Vancouver: Tantalus, 1975).

Quoi Ek Cutting railroaded and bouldered basket case against the Yellow Oath if I had any biased mind to invent lies, or to utter falsehood, the high Heaven, the true God, will punish me, sink me in the river and drown me in the deep sea, forfeit my future generations and cast my soul into hell to suffer for ever and ever the British Columbia Sugar Refining Company sweet talking Chinese Sugar speciously described as British in competition with industry employing white men forty times higher than rice-fed, half-naked, unwashed coolies and B.C. Refined Sugar costs no more than Hongkong Coolie labour sugar if you want to build John's nation you cannot do it by sending your money to Hongkong because B.C. is refined by the most modern methods and processes, operated by white workmen under absolutely sanitary conditions all very well to talk about a white British Columbia but WE can be Orientalized just as thoroughly by using Hongkong sugar as though we let down the barriers and freely admitted our shiftered and greedy pronouns surrounded by Tonto so we[‡] have carpet tacks, thumb tacks, Junior tacks, Super tacks, smoke stacks, patty stacks, hard tack, mactac, well stacked, sewer tax, school tax, sales tax, municipal tax, city tax, provincial tax, federal tax, income tax, and . . . now that you got that head tax will you collect a heart tax too?

[‡] This "tacks" list adapted from Clarence Sihoe's script for "Historical Spoof" as published in *Inalienable Rice,* Powell Street Revue and The Chinese Canadian Writers Workshop, Vancouver, 1979.

a FEW YEARS AGO
I GET HIS GUN.

Sometime after my father dies, when my mother's cleaning out some cupboards she says Freddy you'd better do something about your father's gun. I've never seen it before, never knew he owned one. But apparently he did, for protection, my mom says, when he brought the cash home late at night after closing up. Before the cafe had a safe.

When I take it down to the RCMP station to let them dispose of it I discover it has never been registered, so the Mounties run a check on it. That takes a few months and while I'm waiting I wonder if my father had, in his agitated past, been involved in something shady. Where did he get the gun? Chicago? Was it smuggled in? Opium? Gambling? That's it, he must have won it in Vancouver Chinatown. Or maybe from an Italian up the Gulch in Trail? Suppose they find out the gun's a murder weapon, used in a robbery across the border. This could be a mess, a murder investigation after he's dead. Thank god nothing turns up. I decide to keep it, register it, put it away. I don't want any more checking up. He probably just needed a gun, as Mom said, for protection and, being a Chinaman, he'd have had to get it under the counter, at a pawn shop, that kind of thing.

STRANGE TO WATCH YOUR CHILDREN'S
BLOODS. LIKE ONE

of those sped-up movies of a cell dividing under a microscope. For just a split second your body'll do something Asian—like poised over a dish of lo bok with your chopsticks. There's just a brief Chinese glint in your eyes that flashes some shadow of track across your blond and ruddy Anglo-Swedish dominance. Some uvular word for hunger guttered at the back of your mouth, waiting. Or how about your cousins from Trail, where we gaze at the same sudden trace behind a dark Italian countenance.

And I've watched you both closely at times to see if I can detect any of that Nordic gloom my grandparents brought over from Sweden. Once in awhile during your teenage years I worried that that depressive despair might overwhelm you as it has me from time to time. But what foolish stereotyping, to generalize ethnic property like that.

Certainly your Swedish grandmother has more cheerfulness about her than melancholy. And friends of ours have frequently said, your daughters are really pleasant, smiling all the time, such happy girls. And you've been that way to me, too. So maybe I fret for naught, as usual. Besides you're only as much Swede as I am Chinese, one-quarter, twenty-five percent, a waning moon, a shinplaster, a blind alley, a semi-final, less than half a cup of honey.

And exactly half Brit. Now that's the one I can't figure out. Your mother claims she isn't as strong and tough as I think she is. Rock island North Sea solid English weather fortitude. Sometimes just plain stubbornness, and you both got enough of that.

But oleomargarine soft gets white pulp coloured hydrogenated yellow carotene miscegenated more than real thing and better than butter mommy says for you just Mary baby ladies cream Swede.

*L*AKE LINK. A SMALL BEACH
ETCHED OUT FROM

the breakwater to the north. Driftwood. Broom. Forest on the move. At the top of the beach an old low-limbed cottonwood our daughters call the "moss tree." And just below that, a tripod of blackened driftwood they've totemed Loki, from teeth-brushing down at the lake when they were young. After our dog. Dead now. Loki buried at Smoky Creek. Fiction is impossible, yet moving onto this land secured through my wife's British heritage, I feel at times that I've trespassed into D. H. Lawrence's new Heaven and Earth: "shyly and in homage linger for an invitation." I look for rocks along the shore. Some tableau. Rocks that tell a story I haven't heard before. Rocks I can translate into signals, "disembarked at last."

The problem here is that I am an obstacle. I can't get out of the way now that I've stepped into the frame. Everything's out there larger elsewhere and then I add myself who's watching, who's interloped into this fold of property imagined by power and class as simply the echo of an old empire heaven, who's slipped into this tribal paradigm in a bog of algae, just like the dog.

*M*Y WIFE'S GRANDPARENTS HOMESTEADED

THIS PLACE. HER GRANDFATHER

was a remittance man from England. In 1924 he anchored one of the old sternwheelers (the *Kokanee*) against the pilings and set up a floating hotel for weekend visitors from Nelson and Idaho, as part of his plan to attract retired gentry from the old country, particularly ex-naval officers. In his promotional brochure he reasons with prospective clients about a potential problem:

> The servant problem is a difficult point, but it seems to be so everywhere. In B.C. it is best solved by a Chinese cook. A good Chinaman will do the work of two ordinary maids, but he costs about £120 a year. High as this seems it must be remembered that he is an indefatigable worker. The alternative to a Chinaman is what is often called a "home help." Some girls who go out to do domestic work want to live with the family, and that does not always suit. That is not always the case, however, and sometimes these girls are a great success. After all it is much the same thing in England. Sometimes one is lucky with one's servants, sometimes it is otherwise.

So their cook was a Chinaman. Their girls caught fish for him to cook for the customers. Dolly Varden, trout, kokanee, mud suckers. The Chinaman lived on the boat. A small room in a corner of the lower deck. He fried the fish in butter and served them with boiled potatoes (grown in the garden across the creek) and canned peas and carrots. No salad. For himself he steamed the fish in black bean sauce and something bitter. He always had a pot of rice on the stove.

$\mathcal{I}$ HARDLY EVER GO INTO KING'S
FAMILY RESTAURANT

because, when it comes to Chinese cafes and Chinatowns, I'd rather be transparent. Camouflaged enough so they know I'm there but can't see me, can't get to me. It's not safe. I need a clear coast for a getaway. Invisible. I don't know who I am in this territory and maybe don't want to. Yet I love to wander into Toronto's Chinatown and eat tofu and vegetables at my favourite barbecue joint and then meander indolently through the crowds listening to the tones and watching the dark eyes, the black hair. Sometimes in a store, say, I'm picking up a pair of new kung-fu sandals and the guy checks my Mastercard as I sign and he says Wah! You Chinese? heh heh heh! because he knows I'm not. Physically, I'm racially transpicuous and I've come to prefer that mode.

I want to be there but don't want to be seen being there. By the time I'm ten I'm only white. Until 1949 the only Chinese in my life are relatives and old men. Very few Chinese kids my age. After '49, when the Canadian government rescinds its Chinese Exclusion Act, a wave of young Chinese immigrate to Canada. Nelson's Chinese population visibly changes in the early fifties. In a few years there are enough teenage Chinese kids around to not only form an associa- tion, the Nelson Chinese Youth Association, but also a basketball team. And they're good, too. Fast, smart. I play on the junior high school team and when the NCYA team comes to play us, I know a lot of the Chinese guys. But my buddies at school call them Chinks and geeks and I feel a little embarrassed and don't talk much with the Chinese kids. I'm white enough to get away with it and that's what I do.

But downtown, working in the cafe, things are different. Some of the young guys start working at our cafe and my dad's very involved with helping them all settle into their new circumstances. He acts as an interpreter for a lot of the legal negotiations. Everyone's trying to reunite with long-lost relatives. Anyway, I work alongside some of these new Chinese and become friends.

Shu brings his son over around 1953 and Lawrence is in the cafe business for the rest of his working life. Lawrence and I work together in the Diamond until I leave small-town Nelson for university at the coast. We're good friends. Even today, as aging men, we always exchange greetings whenever we meet on the street. But I hardly ever go into his cafe.

So now, standing across the street from King's Family Restaurant, I know I'd love to go in there and have a dish of beef and greens, but he would know me, he would have me clear in his sights, not Chinese but stained enough by genealogy to make a difference. When Lawrence and I work together, him just over from China, he's a boss's son and I'm a boss's son. His pure Chineseness and my impure Chineseness don't make any difference to us in the cafe. But I've assumed a dull and ambiguous edge of difference in myself; the hyphen always seems to demand negotiation.

I decide, finally, to cross the street. I push myself through the door and his wife, Fay, catches me with the corner of her eye. She doesn't say anything and I wonder if she recognizes me. The white waitress takes my order and I ask if Lawrence is in the kitchen. He is, she says.

I go through Lawrence's kitchen door like I work there. I relish the little kick the door is built to take. He's happy to see me and stops slicing the chicken on the chopping block, wipes his hands on his apron and shakes my hand. How's your mother? Whatchyou doing here? How's Ernie and Donnie? Family, that's what it is. The politics of the family.

He says something to the cook, a young guy. Then he turns to me and says hey Freddy, did you know this is your cousin? He's from the same area near Canton. His name is Quong. Then in Chinese, he gives a quick explanation to Quong; no doubt my entire Chinese family history. Lawrence smiles at me like he used to when were kids: he knows something I don't. I suffer the negative capability of camouflage.

How many cousins do I have, I wonder. Thousands maybe. How could we recognize one another? Names.

The food, the names, the geography, the family history—the filiated dendrita of myself displayed before me. I can't escape, and don't want to, for a moment. Being there, in Lawrence's kitchen, seems one of the surest places I know. But then after we've exchanged our mutual family news and I've eaten a wonderful dish of tofu and vegetables, back outside, on the street, all my ambivalence gets covered over, camouflaged by a safety net of class and colourlessness—the racism within me that makes and consumes that neutral (white) version of myself, that allows me the sad privilege of being, in this white white world, not the target but the gun.

ℐHE POLITICS OF THE FAMILY.♦

♦ Writing is research. Suddenly I'm excited by the possibility of some insight into my desire for camouflage. I go to my bookshelf and grab R.D. Laing's *The Politics of the Family,* that wonderful series of Massey Lectures from 1968. The last lecture is titled "Refractive Images: A World at Large":

> Last week I began to look at a little of the structure of one of the varieties of the Western "conscience". One admires its ingenuity. It must constitute one of the biggest knots in which man has ever tied himself. One of its many peculiar features is that the more tied in the knot, the less aware are we that we are tied in it.
>
> . . .
>
> Anyone fully caught in the full anti-calculus of this kind cannot possibly avoid being bad in order to be good. In order to comply with the rules, rules have to be broken. Even if one could wash out one's brain three times a day, part of one's self must be aware of what one is not supposed to know in order to assure the continuance of those paradoxical states of multiplex ignorance, spun in the paradoxical spiral that the more we comply with the law, the more we break the law: the more righteous we become the deeper our sin; our *righteousness* is as filthy as rags.
>
> . . .

We would rather be anywhere, as long as we are somewhere. We would rather be anyone, as long as we are someone.

ᵀHE CHINESE BANQUET AT
OUR FAMILY REUNION IS

prepared by a few of my cousins and one of my brothers. It's all watched over and orchestrated by Aunty Ethel.

I putter around the community hall kitchen trying to help out a bit and I can't help but notice that Ethel's *chef de confidence* is my brother Donnie, the blondest Asian in our family. Most of my cousins turn red when they drink but Donnie lights up like a Chinatown after rain. He's pretty fair for a Chink.

He's stir-frying the chow mein vegetables on Ray's huge gas-fired wok. I stand over him and ask him how he does this dish. He says he parboiled and drained the noodles, tossed them in peanut oil and then put them in the oven to warm and crisp up just a little. In the wok he started with the sliced chicken, garlic, ginger, and onions. After a few minutes, he says, start adding other vegetables: celery, bok choy, broccoli, bamboo shoots, water chestnuts, black mushrooms, and, right at the end, some bean sprouts and what he calls *wung gee,* a charred-looking tree fungus that's slippery and delicate after being soaked. Season with soy sauce and combine with noodles.

Somehow Donnie's managed to get more recipes out of Ethel than her own kids. Marie says she's even asked Don how to do some of her mother's dishes.

He's too blond to be the best Chinese cook in the family, I think to myself. Brotherly racism? No, just racing after the food—inescapable tastes that seem to have driven him further for the answers to that need than any of us.

I remember coming home late one night as a teenager and finding Donnie, about eight years old and known for his sleepwalking, sitting under the kitchen table in the dark and eating cold, raw, and greasy Chinese sausage. Even today, he keeps a piece of foong cheng in his freezer.

𝒰P FRONT BETWEEN THE
DOOR AND THE SODA

fountain is the till. It's modern, electric and its gears churn with a technical precision that opens the drawer and prints the take on a roll that has to be matched each night with all the green meal checks for the day. This shiny hub sits on a glass display case of cigars and chocolate bars. Only the Americans who come up from Spokane and guys whose wives have babies buy the cigars and once in a while I get one of those metal tubes the expensive Thermidors are packaged in. On top of the glass case, beside the cash register, is a rubber mat for picking up change and a metal spike for the paid checks. To the right of the display case are all the cigarettes, stacked up by brand in specially-built shelving so you pull a pack from the bottom of the stack. One of the cashier's jobs during the lulls is to stock these shelves. I love the colour and polish of the packaging and well-ordered display. One Saturday afternoon I got my first cigarettes from that display, Kools with a picture of a penguin on the pack.

We always have a woman cashier. My mother did it for awhile but my dad didn't like her working in the cafe and he put Miko, the eldest of two young Japanese sisters, on the till. By the time I leave home it's an older woman who has worked in the cafe as a waitress for many years. She's like a friendly gatekeeper up by the front door and knows everyone. The cashier doesn't start until midmorning coffee rush and until then my dad will do the till if change is needed. The customers are regulars and can be trusted to put the right amount on the rubber pad as they leave.

Under the display case we keep a supply of pastel-green check pads, fresh rolls for the cash register, and a cigar box of ious. Thirty years after my dad dies my brother Donnie discovers a box of ious in my mom's cedar chest. Look at this he says. Here's an IOU for two hundred dollars signed by that old skinflint Tom Greenbuck in 1953. Dad helped him out when he was just starting and now he's pretty well off. I guess that's how you do it, by not paying your debts. He's still alive; we should collect from him, Donnie suggests.

IT'S A SMALL COLT
PISTOL. I KEEP IT

in a cigar box and I don't have any bullets. Sometimes I hold it in my hand and think about where it might have been. I think of him walking home on a snowy night over the old bridge across the Columbia in Trail with the money bag under his overcoat and his hand on the pistol in his pocket. Alone.

SOFT ICE CREAM HITS NELSON
ABOUT 1953 BUT

our cafe doesn't have it yet. You need a special machine to make soft ice cream and Wait's News on the corner of the next block gets the first one in town. Walter Wait's a quiet, unassuming guy and he comes into the Diamond for lunch several times a week. But after he gets that soft ice cream machine Walter sometimes rubs it into my dad and asks for soft ice cream for dessert and my dad has to eat crow.

One hot July lunch hour, could be during the midsummer bonspiel, the restaurant's packed and my dad's really running high and fast. He catches Walter off guard and offers him soft ice cream for dessert. Walter's a bit stunned; he thought he had the only soft ice cream around. Anyway, he calls my dad's bluff. My dad goes back through the kitchen, down the back steps, through the alley and across the street to Wait's News where he buys a soft ice cream cone, runs back the same way, puts the ice cream on a Diamond dish, and kicks the door loudly in his rush up to the front counter where he places in front of Walter his dish of soft ice cream dessert. Everyone up at the front counter looks at Walter. He can't believe his eyes. My dad breaks out into a huge grin and then laughs like hell as Walter digs in. I think he even charges him for it.

BETWEEN ELEVEN AND NOON A LULL IN BUSINESS

allows us to get things ready for the rush. We fill the butter trays, move clean dishes and cutlery to the station at the back of the cafe and under the counters up front, get the dessert custards and deep apple pies into the glass coolers, insert the day's specials into the menus, and generally tidy up and get ship shape, as my dad calls it. The kitchen help and any Chinese who work out front usually eat their rice meal around eleven, something special Shu has put together, usually some soup of greens with salt fish on the side. This is one of those times of day when we can relax a bit, talk to each other, kid around.

I sit down with him for a few minutes in the last booth while he's eating his rice. We talk about him and George Kaiway forming a team with my friend Gordie and myself for the Butterfly Bonspiel in Creston in March. We talk about how the Rangers, my team in the bantam league, is doing. We talk about when I'm going to shovel Pearson's sidewalks today. We talk about maybe driving over to Trail during the holidays. We talk about what shifts I'm going to work next week.

We hardly ever talk about him. I never ask him who he is or where he's from. He's just there, with his shirt sleeves rolled half way up his forearms, a package of Players in his right shirt pocket and pens and his glasses case bulging the other, frowning, scolding, kidding, laughing, wondering. That's the big Pro noun Him, driving straight ahead through the day, this weird food that's never on the menu, rocket fuel.

My Dad's Favourite Song on the Jukebox Is

Frankie Lane's "Mule Train." I ask him, when it's not that busy and I decide to play three up for a dime, to choose a piece. He says play that one with the big crack of the whip in it.

His taste in stuff like music and movies is really hard to figure. I know he'll take my mother to a dance at the Lion's Club. But he hardly ever goes to movies. I don't think I've ever seen him read a book, though my mom gets the Book of the Month. And all of us kids do a bit of music: school band, piano lessons, pop forty-fives.

And I don't think I've ever seen him get through a television pro-gramme; he always falls asleep within ten minutes of sitting down in his La-Z-Boy.

He's attracted to the bizarre. At the fall fair he does the freak show first, always commenting on the snake lady. One year the cir-cus has Siamese twins and he goes to see them several times. He's in awe. And his preferred cartoon is "Ripley's Believe It or Not." He'll say hey! Jee-zus christ, they've found a lost tribe of pygmies in the Amazon. Look at that, they've got big sticks in their noses!

Whenever we talk about travel, the fantasy trip-of-a-lifetime, he says he'd like to go to Africa. And his favourite animal is the ele-phant. Old Mr. Pearson, just down the street, collects miniature ele-phants and my dad admires and contributes to his collection.

He seems to regard animals from some distance, as almost exter-nal to his world. When we go to the Stanley Park Zoo he never smiles at the animals but frowns at their mysteriousness. When he goes, infrequently, on a weekend hunting trip with some of the boys, he does all the cooking and just walks around in the bush with them, no gun.

Fishing is a different matter. He'll look at me with his serious brown eyes like I'm crazy when I catch a fish, and give out a surprised laugh. I wonder what gets to him fishing in the Columbia River at Trail, after work, along the rocks, swift-flowing mind emptying. Or off in the creek on a Sunday afternoon picnic, cousins and uncles, a ball game.

One summer day my brother Ernie and I and a friend hike out the Great Northern tracks to Apex to fish in Cottonwood Creek. He packs us a lunch: apple pie, chocolate bars, an orange, and a can of beans. We fish the creek all afternoon and then he drives out after work in his turquoise Ford and finds us. We haven't caught anything all day so he puts on an old pair of boots, tucks his dress pants into his socks, and gets his rod out of the car. He wants us to catch a fish. I can tell he really wants us to feel the sudden blip of success when a fish bites.

When I fish now sometimes, his body extends out of me holding the rod, fingers on the line just so, glassy gaze, vertical invisible layers, the line going deep into the lake or flung out onto the surface glaze of river current, layers of darkness, invisible fish, fading.

a NEW MENU EVERY DAY.
SOUP DU JOUR

(my first French has the cachet of crumpled crackers): vegetable, cream of mushroom, beef barley, chicken noodle, cream of tomato, navy bean (my favourite), and clam chowder for Friday. There's also the choice of canned soup, Campbell's, which has its own special brushed chrome display and electric soup heater up in the front section (only seldom will we sell anything from this display, night shift maybe, after the beer parlours close).

The list of specials is always the same except the first on the list will change each day. Hot roast beef sandwich on Monday, sausages with gravy and mashed potatoes on Tuesday, beef stew on Wednesday, pork chops on Thursday, some kind of fish on Friday, maybe Salisbury steak on Saturday, and prime rib of beef, roast pork, or roast turkey on Sunday. I'm partial to Shu's chicken pot pie but he doesn't make it that often. Each of these specials comes with soup, bread, coffee or tea, and dessert of Jell-O, deep apple pie, custard, or, on Sunday, a dish of ice cream.

Below the daily specials are the entrées. Various steaks, mixed grill, breaded veal cutlets (with a light but spicy tomato sauce, uhm!), fish and chips, half-a-dozen fried oysters, and so forth. At the bottom of the page the desserts, soft drinks, tea, coffee, and so forth.

This is the daily menu and it's attached with a paper clip inside the pastel-green regular menu which has a complete listing of sandwiches, steaks, soda fountain, and Chinese food. On the front of the regular menu is a picture of Nelson taken from Gyro Park lookout, a picture of trees, progress, a cushioning valley, streets gridded gently down to the lake.

I'm intrigued by the mechanics of production (an early seed of my interest in publishing?). In the back office the menu's typed using a heavily inked ribbon. The original sheet is offset onto a rubbery-hard gelatinous surface in a nine by twelve cake pan by rubbing it thoroughly with your hand. You can lift about forty copies of purple type from that surface before it dims. When you finish you have to put the jellied plate back into the walk-in cooler.

On Christmas Day and New Year's Day we use special paper and, by changing the ribbon in the typewriter, we're able to get red and green colours. Now that I think of it, that must have been how the gamblers printed the Chinese lottery tickets, in one of those baking pans. Lucky red green cranberry sauce, a good luck year, eat all you want, smile, leave a tip.

$\mathscr{I}$'M NOT AWARE IT'S CALLED TOFU UNTIL AFTER

I leave home. It's one of those ingredients that are transparent to me in the multitude of Cantonese dishes I grow up eating. So, until my dad tells me what that white stuff is called, I'm unable to order it during my forays into Vancouver Chinatown. Even when I first try it out on a waitress, she looks puzzled and says something in Chinese to her father who's hanging out by the till. She comes back to my booth and says o.k., you mean dow-uw foo, bean curd!

But over the past forty years, tofu has come into its own in North America, taking a choice place among the burgeoning macrobiotic and cholesterol-conscious diet fads. Available at any supermarket. If I'd been smart in the sixties I would have invested in soybean futures. There's even a little hippie tofu industry that has sprung up to supply the organic craze marketed through local co-ops. I wear my Kootenay Tofu T-shirt with pride.

This is all to my delight because tofu is, after rice, basic to my culinary needs. I've rendered this custard-like cake from pureed soybeans; I've pressed it, frozen it, mashed it, and cubed it; I've boiled, steamed, fried and marinated it; I even use Tofunaise as a substitute for mayonnaise. One summer I planted soybeans with some improbable fantasy of building my own tofu from the ground up. My attraction to this food is more than belief; it's a deep need, obsessive.

My basic all-time favourite dish is braised bean curd with vegetables. Cut each cake of tofu into one-inch cubes and very gently stir-fry along with some chopped green onion until the outer surface is lightly browned and the cake holds together without crumbling. Add some sliced vegetables: bok choy, carrots, green or red pepper, whatever you have around. Black Chinese mushrooms and water chestnuts are a nice option. As the dish is finishing, stir in a couple tablespoons of soy sauce and then some cornstarch mixed in water for thickening. This tasty and nutritious melange is spooned over steamed rice and washed down with oolong tea. There. That's a lunch.

THE VINYL FLOOR IN THE CAFE HAS TO

be swept at least twice a day. We sprinkle some kind of granular stuff on it that's supposed to keep the dust down while we sweep.

One day, though, one of our regulars just gets up and walks out without finishing her stewed oysters because I'm sweeping the floor. She complains to my dad that I'm raising the dust and it's getting in her food. He tells me I shouldn't sweep when she's in the place.

Betty Goodman usually has cinnamon toast for morning coffee break. She lives with her mother in the Annabel Apartments building and her family owns Goodman's Furniture just down the street. My dad says they're Jews, the only ones in town. Betty's the first Jew I meet and I cast her as a mysterious survivor. I try to locate her in post-war comic book stereotypes but they're all Germans and Americans and I can't find anything about the Jews there. The library isn't much help either. Bunch of religious stuff, not the war stories of the German massacre of the Jews my dad talks about.

When I have to deliver something to her at the apartment building, I walk through the halls and I'm intrigued by the cooking smells, pungent with frying chops, cabbage, so different from the food smells at our house. Yet the same, too, because it's about five o'clock Saturday and I can hear Foster Hewitt's voice coming from nearly every apartment door I pass announcing the start of that night's game. Familiar, yet different.

𝒴OU GET TO KNOW THE
TIPPERS. IF THEY

sit in your section you go for them and you give them top service. Some customers'll even tip just for a cup of coffee.

One woman, actually the first tip I ever get, always tips more than her check. She usually just has coffee and toast or something small that might cost about thirty-five cents. Then she leaves forty cents in change on the table tucked under the saucer.

Another woman tips only me. If someone else waits her she won't tip. Just me. She and I know that and I always try to get her. Who can figure?

One old man comes in for breakfast every morning and never tips. But then last Christmas he gives me an envelope with five bucks in it.

There's a real honour code between the waiters and waitresses. If you clean off a table you're supposed to hand over the tip to the server. I remember one girl who didn't last long at our cafe because she was always lifting tips.

At the end of a shift sometimes I empty my pockets in the last booth. I show my dad and he says that's good Freddy, you work hard and you get lots of tips. He grins. But I don't see past that grin until years later. You know, more than likely, a little bait for the boy.

*T*HE RUSH HOUR AT LUNCH TODAY IS MORE

intense than usual because of the Christmas shopping. People have come into Nelson from the outlying areas so the cafe is full of both regulars and others; there's a lineup at the door. Everyone's tracked in snow and the floor is so wet by the till we have to mop it up. The big window up front is steamed over and the place noisy with dishes and the repetitive kicking of the kitchen door.

He has a heady seasonal feeling with all the business and excitement. He greets people he hasn't seen for a year, tells them to just wait a minute and he'll have a table cleaned up for them. He usually gets them seated and when it's really busy like now he'll call over Donna or someone else to wait on them.

Bert Herridge, the local CCF MP, has just come in on the train from Ottawa for his Christmas break and he's politicking around the booths on a first-name basis.

Charlie Bing's son, recently returned from the Korean War, walks in the front door of the Diamond. This is unusual. Old Mr. Walsh, one of the town's most patriotic Legionnaires, insists that Eddie Bing sit on the stool next to him so they can talk army. Eddie's one of the few Chinese kids to grow up in Nelson and if he wasn't wearing that uniform we all know that he wouldn't be walking in the front door and getting this kind of attention.

Bob Philips, a regular, peeks in, sees the crowd, and says to Fred he'll grab something later.

Today's rush starts to calm down around two o'clock but the cafe stays busy all afternoon, right into the supper hour. Fred usually runs home after the lunch hour to get a clean shirt and fresh socks and shoes but today he stays on well into the supper hour. And tomorrow will be even heavier. But he's happy at this time of year. Both he and the cafe glitter.

*Y*OU NEVER TAUGHT ME HOW,
BUT I REMEMBER

your frown, particularly that, your frown, whenever you confronted
something new in your world, like our basement, how to move
around the furnace, or a gun, how to aim it, or logging, say, how Tak
Mori's caulk boots sound on the running board of his deep-green
Fargo pickup, or, better still, your scowl of incredulity at how to
gulp quickly Granny Erickson's Christmas pickled herring while
her beak-nosed challenge sat in the kitchen chair opposite your dark
bird-eyed defiance (oof dah) or when Betty Goodman ordered
stewed oysters for lunch and you got me to wait on her while you
went to the can and puked, all those puzzled moments in the new
world when your brown brow squinched up while you translated
vectors or politesse or measurement or celebration or strange foods
or weird Europeans or, through gold-rimmed reading glasses, the
day's page one world wars page two Baker Street page five sports
Nelson Daily News spread out over the gray Formica table top in the
back booth of the Diamond Grill, all these moments nothing but
your river of truth, fiction, and history, nothing but the long nights
of a Chinese winter waiting for the promised new/old world of
mothers fathers brothers sisters, river of ocean, river of impossible
passing, too large and formidable even later spinning your days out
under Elephant Mountain such encounters with possibility criss-
crossed on your forehead, indeed, your whole body wired taut for
daily brushes with what, the foreign, that jailed Juan de Fuca immigrant in your eyes as you looked, now look out to the sea this sentence makes, puzzled, cryptic, wild, bewildered, exed and perplexed
thought so far away and other, but then your lower lip bites up
under your teeth, hands, fingers, eyes, laughing, how, to. . . .

But then you by now, like everyone else in town, we've all, walked past the sign in the window of the Club Cafe—

SPECIAL CHRISTMAS DINNER

$1.50

ALL THE TRIMMINGS

—the same Christmas dinner Sammy Wong has cooked every year since he bought the Club in 1938 from his cousin who went back to China to find a girl. Sammy didn't. Never bought or brought a wife. Only girls he knows are his waitresses and Edna has been there the longest; she's a steam-boat and makes sure Sammy keeps the place tiptop. She pretty much runs the front of the cafe. So, even the sign, she probably made that, a few sprigs of holly coloured with a green wax crayon and "All the Trimmings" in red, sits now getting stained from the condensation running down the window in the heated steamy and smoky cafe. The only thing Edna doesn't like about his Christmas dinner, and she tells him, too, is that special cranberry sauce he makes every year, you're not gonna make that again, it's too tart, the jellied canned stuff is nicer, sweeter, darker. Sammy just glares at her from over the stove. He thinks, tart? All time I make this—what's a matter with you?

Just across the street the New Grand Hotel has a sprayed-icing window stencilled in with "Season's Greetings." Their dining room will be closed Christmas Day but for New Year's Eve the hotel is holding a gala banquet and dance. For this, hotel magnate Dominic Rissuti, the cigar-smoking rotund president of the Columbo Lodge and local nickel Mafiosi, has hired the Melodaires who do mostly popular songs like "Mocking Bird Hill." (Their saxophonist, Lefty Black, regularly swoons a lot of the town's women with his lilting rendition of "Deep Purple.") For eight dollars a couple you get a sit-down dinner with a choice of ham, roast beef, or grilled salmon steak, a bar that opens at 6:30 (drinks three for a dollar), noisemakers, and a glass of special punch to welcome in the New Year. All this come-on appears on a big display ad that has bubbles rolling out of glasses on page two of the *Nelson Daily News*. The only problem Rissuti has run into is getting a liquor license because New Year's Eve falls on a Sunday this year. In Al's Barber Shop next door he complains to some of the guys, That goddamned police chief says he won't sign the license. What do I gotta do? Go to the mayor?

Eadie Petrella, the owner of the Shamrock Grill (gauze curtains, no juke box), never could figure out how Lok Pon managed to get his turkey so moist (fifteen years cooking in logging camps) but what he remembers is that first Christmas he worked for her she came into the kitchen and watched over him all morning garumphing around while he filled and trussed and basted, no smile, no talk, particularly the no talk, she usually talks non-stop, at least in the kitchen to the waitresses, always babbling something he can't understand anyway, so now, after six years of cooking at the Shamrock, he watches her cocked over his stove testing his gravy, smacking her lips, eyeing the three birds he's cooked racked over the warming oven, and her eyes pinch slightly with an mmmm (he knows it's good) and she turns away with a haughty Better get those Brussels sprouts started! not to him but to his half-wit helper and dishwasher so he's left standing there by the steam table with lots to do yet and curses her under his breath—You mucka high!

Except, by the time the holidays are over we've all, even at the Diamond Grill where the plum puddings with rum and maple sauce continue in high demand, we've had enough of turkey and ham and stuffing and mashed potatoes and know that the real gung hay fa choy Chinese New Year's celebration sometime in January will bring on the Diamond's legendary Chinese banquet with local high muckamucks like the mayor, a few aldermen, the police chief and fire chief, steadies like the early-morning pensioners and CPR shift

workers and cab drivers, even the waitresses set places for their husbands or boyfriends in the booths disguised now with white table-
cloths and dishes of quarters wrapped in red wrapping paper and
lichee nuts, both chopsticks and cutlery, bottles of scotch and rye,
this once-a-year feast tops the whole season as far as I'm concerned
starting even with birds-nest soup and then the dishes come too fast,
barbecue pork, chicken and almond chop suey (incredible washed
down with Canada Dry gingerale), beef and green pepper, snow
peas, fried rice, steamed rice, deep fried rock cod, abalone, jumbo
shrimp and black beans finished off with ice cream or Jell-O and lots
of left-over Christmas cake and a few speeches even the mayor's
toast to the shy Chinese cooks who stand just outside the swinging
kitchen door in their dirty aprons faces glazed with sweat, Shu Ling
Mar the chief cook looks to you and says something in Chinese and
you translate He says please come back again you're all welcome,
lots more in the kitchen! Then somehow, all that mess disappears
and the floors are washed by six the next morning when you open
up.

Then what is that taste, mulled memory, kitchen sediment. Your
hands and body fill, pour, stir. Dark brown eyes the Aleutian land
bridge over the stove—and dancing. How do I make your tangy
sauce for seafood cocktail so good my mouth waters in this sentence
saying ketchup horseradish lemon Tabasco maybe a dash of soy.
Something gave pure zip. Your shoulders. I thought the sharp, red
bottle in the top cupboard. Reach. Was crabmeat. Even something
creamy crunchy celery tomatoed and all that spooned into short,
glasses, fluted what I thought were like sundae dishes first lined
with a lettuce leaf a few dozen made up in advance and kept on a
shelf in the walk-in cooler. I'd sneak one. Or two. Boston Cream pie
on a slack and snowy Sunday afternoon. Where did that taste for
such zip Charlie-chim-chong-say-wong-lung-chung come to your
mouth in a shot shout as you clicked your tongue eyes sparkled if it
was too hot too much kick they'd water a bit and you'd cut the sauce

with what, HP, or maybe that other dark brown steak sauce A-1 under the counters by the cutlery trays. Not cayenne. No, that was never your spice. Chili powder. You looked more Mexican than Chinese and I thought fiction could have made you Filipino. So, of course, chili or Tabasco. But of yours, something with more smack than gut, not pepper, further forward on the palate to match the sea brine but with bang, Oooo-Eee, the boot to begin every banquet and Chinese New Year. That now then is winter lingulate imprint in December. Under the breath. Just outside. Massive dark hole swirl of oriental nebulae, just outside. Or just next door, the mayor, the pool hall, anyone else, everyone else. And all time. What's a matter? You just smiled, laughed and said Pretty good gung hey, eh Freddy? Fa choy! That's how.

$\mathcal{B}$ESIDES THE FOUR MINIATURE
WURLITZERS STATIONED ON THE

front horseshoe counters, there's also a juke box in each booth along the wall. The big floor model Wurlitzer with all its lights, revolving record caddie, and mechanized arms and platters, is up against the wall between the counter section and the booths.

On quiet winter Sunday afternoons, snow gusting around a deserted Baker Street outside, only the odd customer, I fiddle around with one of the Wurlitzers on the second counter.

They're great little machines. You turn the flaps that list the songs by flipping a little spring-loaded handle on top. The letters, A to H, and the numbers, one to eight, are on two rows of pushbuttons along the bottom. Sometimes I manage to jimmy one of them open and get at the nickels, which I just recycle through the juke box. Or, three for a dime.

I play songs according to the mood of the cafe, specific to certain customers. Like if there's a family with kids messing around in their raspberry Jell-O I'll play Patti Page singing "How Much Is That Doggie In the Window." My mom likes that one too, pretty upbeat. And I think of her whenever "Mockin' Bird Hill" comes up.

If I have some work to do like carting dishes back and forth to the kitchen I punch in "Blue Tango" or "Happy Wanderer." It feels good to have a rhythm to work by. One of the songs everyone likes to hear a lot of is "Tennessee Waltz"; feels like weekend dances down at the IODE Hall or out at Ymir or Salmo. "Goodnight Irene" is another favourite and it always makes me think of Uncle Gus and Aunty Irene.

There's this woman who comes in every Sunday afternoon and orders tea and a grilled cheese sandwich. I think she plays the organ at one of the churches. Anyway, she never smiles and always sits for a long time looking into her teacup. I play "Auf Wiedersehn Sweetheart" or "Until I Waltz With You" two or three times in a row. She seems to like that and always leaves a tip.

Those quiet Sunday afternoons I just sit there on that stool up by the soda fountain and stare out the large window at the snow and the red brick Gilker building across the street listening to The Four Aces croon out "Tell Me Why" or "Cry" by Johnny Ray. "On Top of Old Smoky" seems to fit right into living in Nelson and staring across the lake at Elephant Mountain every dreary winter day. At home I listen to jazz but here in the cafe I let myself ease up on serious music and just flow with the moods of the juke box.

WHO IS HE, THIS GUY WITH SMILES AND

a suit coming in the front door of the cafe, eyeing my dad, shaking his hand? Never seen him before. Not in Trail or Nelson. They laugh and talk Chinese as dad grabs a coffee and steers him to a booth near the back. They deal. There are papers and money on the table. Dad signs something and then licks an envelope. They go into the kitchen and you can hear the loud talking and laughter behind the swinging doors.

Can this be the infamous Charley Chim Chong Say Wong Liu Chung my dad was always singing about?

Charley's from Kamloops.

Charley's going back to China.

Charley's going to get a wife.

Charley's going to my dad's village and he's going to deliver a bank draft my dad has given him to some relatives still there.

Charley's going to buy some jade in Hong Kong for my father to give to my mother for Christmas. He'll be gone for a year so he'll post it from Hong Kong. The day it arrives at the restaurant, three months later, my father's excited. He puts the onion-skin letter with red marks and Chinese characters aside and opens a small box of jade and gold rings and earrings and shows them to me with great pride and says jade's so lucky and your mother's going to love it so don't tell her about this it's a surprise.

Charley comes back. China is so far away.

$\mathscr{T}$HE GATES TO THE KITCHEN
ARE THE SAME

gates inside out. Any waitress worth her tips knows it. If you lift someone else's tip when you're cleaning tables, you'll get the gate. Look out! Coming through! You mucka hi! Hinges sprung, springing. In mah-jong the Chief casts two dice to open the gate. When the Kampus Kings play Playmor Junction at New Year's, we split the gate and then cut out past Beasley Bluffs along the snow-blown roads back to town. Slip and slide through the gate of another year. Gung hey fa choy! They swing and they turn, gate of to and gate of from, entrance and exit, the flow, the discharge, the access, the egress, the Mountains of the Blest, the winds of ch'i, mouth of Yin and eye of Yang, the Liver, the Stomach, the core and the surface, the rock and the lake. These are the gates and you can either kick them open or walk through in silence. Same dif.

*J*UST ANOTHER TIGHT LIPPED HIGH
MUCKAMUCK RECEPTION LISTENING

to the whining groans of an old-fart pink-faced investor worried about the Hong Kong real estate takeover, a wincing glance as he moans that UBC has become the University of a Billion Chinks, tense shoulder scrunch as I'm introduced, with emphasis on the Wah, to his built-and-fought-for-inheritor-of-the-country arrogant, raised-eyebrow, senior executive entrepreneur boss pig business associate—so that sometimes my cast of frown-furled brow looks right on past a bent nail, eyes screwed over the lake, into some trees, the tangle of bush impenetrable before they clear cut birch bark pocked crop settin' chokers'd break yer ass so fast you wouldn't even wanna look at a goddamned tree let alone cut through the crap backoff this Havoc old Hav Ok will stuff it in your cry this magic leaping tree will never be the apple of anyone else's eye because this is the last stand which for you is just a weekend pick-em-up truck so fuck the Husky Tower hustle and the Sleepy R train games this rusty nail has been here forever in fact the real last spike is yet to be driven.

*W*HO AM I I THOUGHT I MIGHT SAY

to my friend Charlie Chim Chong Say Wong Liu Chung, the Chinese poet. He said he could tell me more about my father than I can imagine.

Like my name. This Chinese doctor I go to for acupuncture always gets it wrong. He calls me Mah. And I say no, it's Wah. Then he smiles, takes out his pen and writes my characters on my forearm, sometimes on my back, between the needles, or down my leg (sciatic signature). He says Wah just means overseas Chinese. So I'm just Fred Overseas.

I tell him my dad was really Kuan Wah Soon. He says my family comes from Canton region. Then he smiles. He knows so much.

Now I have a large coloured portrait of Kuan Yü, illustrious Chinese ancestor hero of China's epic drama, the *San Kuo*. You can see him as any number of small porcelain or clay statues in Chinatown; he has three long beards swirling out from his chin and cheeks. Charlie says he wasn't even Chinese, probably an invading Moor.

No warlike nomad left in this long, slow stroke of signing and signature. Unreadable, but repeatable.

*J*UK IS A SOUP WE ALWAYS HAVE AFTER

New Year's because it's made with left-over turkey. I think of it as the bridge between our white Christmas (presents and turkey stuffing) and our Chinese New Year (firecrackers and juk). As far as I know, all of the Wah families have it and each is distinctive. Aunty Ethel's is pretty good but my mom still makes my dad's version once in awhile, though neither she nor Ethel add that little shot of rye whiskey he said was the secret to a really good juk. I couldn't taste liquor but boy his soup was the best, a real treat. But he also used the little red dates, which I'd pick aside; they're too much of a contrast, a little too sweet for the full-bodied ricey broth, and Ethel says you don't really need them.

But if you want to try them, get a package of small red pitted dates at the Chinese supermarket. Also, buy only the smallest package of chung toy (salted turnip) since you only need a couple of pieces. For the fu juk (dried bean curd) you'll have to decide between flat sheets or ropes; I prefer the ropes because they're chewier. Soak the whole package of juk overnight. Be sure to wash the chung toy, it's heavily salted. Peel and slice a few fresh water chestnuts. Optional is a bit of the dark seaweed and a few soaked Chinese mushrooms. Put all this with a couple of cups of rice into the turkey stock (you should have about 6–8 cups of liquid). and cook slowly for an hour or so, until the rice is overdone. If not very much of the turkey made it this far and you feel the need for some meat, you can add a bit of sliced pork steak. In the end you should have a thickish gruel, almost a congee.

Juk is even better than bird's-nest soup, though both soups share an intrinsic proprioceptive synapse: memory. While slurping a bowl of juk with the January snow still swirling outside, the memory of the bird itself, only a few weeks old, triangulates with a smoky star-filled night in China. Likewise, with the gelatinous bird's-nest soup, the taste carries images of men climbing the walls of dark caves in Yunan collecting the spaghetti-like translucent strands of bird's nests, the frightened cries of the swallows themselves as piercing as a foreign language.

$\mathcal{T}$HE NAME'S ALL I'VE HAD

TO WORK THROUGH.

What I usually get at a counter is the anticipatory pause after I spell out H. Is that it? Double U AY AYCH? I thought it might be *Waugh*. What kind of name is that, *Wah?* Chinese I say. I'm part Chinese. And she says, boy you could sure fool me. You don't look Chinese at all.

Some of my New England friends pronounce it Fred *War*. One of them, a poet from Massachussetts, liked to play with my name. He'd say, during the Vietnam War in the sixties, Wah, you should go to War! We should nuke those Chinks! That's when I decided I'd never be an American *We*.

I had to book a plane ticket over the phone in Montreal and when I went to pick it up I noticed they'd made it out in the name of Fred *Roy*. The flight attendant even asked if I was related to the Canadiens goal tender, Patrick Roy.

An Okanagan poet I know sometimes addresses envelopes to me with a comic strip cutout of some kid yelling a big cloud *WAH!*

Another Canadian poet, whose books are always alphabetized close to mine at the bottom of the bookshelf, has a line that goes "So. So. So. Ah—to have a name like *Wah*."

And the junk mail addressed to Fred *Wan*, Fred *Way*, Fred *Wash*, Fred *Wag*, Fred *Wan*, Fred *What* is always a semiotic treat. The one that really stopped me in my tracks though was the Christmas card from a tailor in Hong Kong addressed to Fred *Was*.

CELLARS ARE COMPLICIT WITH
GRAVITY. AN ENTIRE TOWN'S

castoffs fall down basement stairs and are recuperated, or not, years later. These middens of bric-a-brac turn, every so slowly, out of mind's sight, and, surely by chance, some anamnestic rhizome will surface briefly and offer itself as an agent of memory. Dust off the spider webs and who knows, the neural orgasm of images might even breed some writing.

So it seems when I gave a reading of some of my poetry one night in Nelson in the early 1980s. After the reading a young woman came up to me and said I didn't know you were involved with the Diamond Grill! We were cleaning up in the basement of a house we're renting and came across an old painted sign that says *Seasons Greetings from the Diamond Grill.* We haven't thrown it out yet; would you like to have it?

THE NEW STAR IS ACTUALLY
OUR FIRST CAFE

in Nelson. We buy into the L.D. Cafe and change the name to the New Star just as Mao's victory north of the Yangze becomes palpable. But there are too many partners, too much trouble, and after a couple of years Dad sells his share.

But between cafes, before actually moving on to the Diamond, he and Mom decide to take the first real holiday of their life. During several weeks one summer we drive south through Spokane and then follow the Columbia River to its mouth. My dad really wants to go through Walla Walla, Washington, just because of the name. We stay in motels with kitchen facilities so we can cook our own food and save a little money. But this is the land of plenty, after the war, and Dad gives us kids each a daily allowance for Tootsie Rolls and baseball bubble gum. Mom buys a few clothes and Dad gets a pair of real alligator shoes in Portland.

Before coming back to Nelson we spend a couple of weeks in Vancouver and meet a lot of different Chinese people and eat out at many Chinese restaurants. Dad goes salmon fishing and scores.

For me the trip is a major embellishment of geography. For him, place never seems to be important. He looks out at it but he never seems to care if he's there or not.

But he loves the sun. He'll go outside for that. He comes down to Lakeside Park after work in the summer and we all meet Mom with her picnic supper. He takes off his shirt and socks and stretches out on the blanket in the warmth his working body, his brown skin smooth from cafe grease and smoke. He closes his eyes and rests an arm across his brow. He seems to sink out of this world into some other, exclusively his, subaudible whisper of a light breeze across a rice paddy, falls asleep into the sky of the water he looks at all day long, plants his fist of rice shoots down and down into the mud dream of green large human connection a terrain to give colour to the water and the place tabled.

𝓗IS FW SIGNET RING ON MY LEFT LITTLE

finger. He wore it on his ring finger. My mother gave it to me for my birthday, years after he died. His watch and his ring were his only daily jewelry. Tie pins and cuff links were just trinkets, gift ornaments. The ring was part of his cool, his click, his body.

Silver initials capped with a triangle that holds a small diamond on a black onyx base set in a rectangle of fourteen karat gold held on the sides by three filigreed leaves.

The hand is such a signifier anyway, with its management of the body's bent, never still with snap and curl, fingers drum and shape intent, brief sleight and flash of knuckle shine, half-moon fingernail, sure dexterous grasp of knife to quick iterated chop of onion, water chestnut under bent fingers, palm held chicken cleavered.

His ring means gabardine, gold, shoes shined, and body on the move with work to do, food to flip, till to punch, pen to write, nose to pick, ball to throw, car to steer, paper to read, coffee to drink, other hands to hold.

𝓗 IS HALF-DREAM IN THE STILL-
DARK BREATHING SILENCE IS

the translation from the bitter-green cloudiness of the winter melon soup in his dream to the sweet-brown lotus root soup he knows Shu will prepare later this morning for the Chinese staff in the cafe. He moves the taste of the delicate nut-like lotus seeds through minor degrees of pungency and smokiness to the crunchy slices of lotus root suspended in the salty-sweet beef broth. This silent rehearsal of the memory of taste moves into his mind so that the first language behind his closed eyes is a dreamy play-by-play about making beef and lotus root soup. Simple: a pound of short ribs and a pound of lotus root in a small pot of water with some soy sauce and salt, a little sliced ginger, maybe a few red Chinese dates. Shu will surely touch it with a piece of dried tangerine peel because it's close to Christmas. He feels his tongue start to move as his mouth waters at the palpable flavour of words.

YEARS IN THE NEVER-ENDING
AFTERSHOCK REVERBERATE ON AT

the margins of perception, decode the fibres of genetic riprap along the biopaths of the ree-mind, turn out the light in ee-light, chain out analogues, undreamed-of switching devices, mirrors, and dreams, track the taste engrams as if they're both nowhere and everywhere, court the cortex, gaze the maze, count the kick, swing the gate, hyphen the blood, unhinge the heart, face to face, eye to open eye.

*H*e usually parks behind the
cafe. Coming down

the hill he crosses Baker Street, turns left behind Wood Vallance Hardware, drives halfway down the alley, manoeuvres around some garbage cans, and noses into his parking spot by a loading dock.

> *Fred Wah*
> *Diamond Grill*
> *Private*

is painted on the dirty cement wall. He climbs the wooden steps to the back door of the cafe and holds open the spring-hinged screen door with his left foot while he unlocks both the dead bolt and a padlock. The smoky glass in the top half of this door is covered by a heavy metal grill and, as he jars it open with a slight body-check, the door clangs and rattles a noisy hyphen between the muffled winter outside and the silence of the warm and waiting kitchen inside.

Afterword

RE-MIXED: THE COMPOUND COMPOSITION
OF *Diamond Grill*

This title references several terms that seem crucial factors to both the imaginary surrounding the discourse of hybridity and the compositional stance I've come to adopt in my writing practice, most specifically to the biofiction *Diamond Grill*.

"To compound" means, basically, to combine, to mix. I'm thinking of it here more in the sense of building, by adding to, much in the way we compound phrases in constructing a complex sentence. And, since *Diamond Grill* is, apparently, prose, the sentence, as a basic unit of composition, offers a useful site in which to explore the dynamics of compounding.

I also have in mind that notion from music remixing of "alteration." I see it as an active and generative re-naming in its inclusion of that typically academic appositive colon in the title, the particularity of the non-centred *punctum* (Roland Barthe on photography) so useful to the kind of compounding I try to explore in much of my writing.

The "re-" is an aspect of a larger poetics, the applied methodology of re-writing, re-cuperating, re-siting and re-citing, re-furbishing, and so forth. It attends to an important aspect of all writing, but particularly poetry and its obsession with song and rhythm, iteration: re-peat, re-iterate. For me this appears in the 70s and 80s "re-reading and re-writing strategies generated in the ethnic and feminist rejections of assimilation, the bargaining for a position in the reterritorialization of inherited literary forms and language" (*Faking It*, p.203). Daphne Marlatt's book, *Salvage* (1991), for example, is a good example of this "re-" poetics in that it "*re-reads* and *re-envisions* [her] earlier writings in light of her feminist experiences of the late 80s and in doing so salvages them" (jacket blurb).

But the most important cipher in this title for me, is that little dash, almost transparent, camouflaged, between those big words RE and

MIX, the HYPHEN. *Diamond Grill*, as you might know, is largely about hybridity, literally about being racially mixed, miscegenated, Asian, Swedish, Scots, ChineseHYPHENCanadian. That hyphen is a real problem for multiculturalism; it's usually a sign of impurity and it's frequently erased as a reminder that the parts, in this case, are not equal to the whole (see p.53, BETTER WATCH OUT FOR THE CRAW . . .). I've written about the hyphen critically in an essay called "Half-Bred Poetics":

> "Yes, the Diamond Grill was a real restaurant. It was on Baker Street in Nelson and was owned by Fred's father. There are a lot of long time Nelson residents who can remember eating there. Fred grew up in Nelson and spent, as you will note in the book, a lot of time in his father's cafe. The storefront that was the cafe in the 40s and 50s is now an optometrist's office (543 Baker Street, I believe)."
>
> Deb Thomas, Librarian,
> Nelson Public Library.

Though the hyphen is in the middle, it is not in the centre. It is a property marker, a boundary post, a borderland, a bastard, a railroad, a last spike, a stain, a cypher, a rope, a knot, a chain (link), a foreign word, a warning sign, a head tax, a bridge, a no-man's land, a nomadic, floating magic carpet, now you see it now you don't. The hyphen is the hybrid's dish, the mestiza's whole-wheat tortillas [Anzaldua 194], the Métis' apple (red on the outside, white on the inside), the happa's egg (white out, yellow in), the mulatto's café au lait. (*Faking It*, p.73)

and in this little poem, more specifically in reference to Canada's Chinese–Canadian history:

How voice the silent dash? Say blindfold, hinge, thorn, spike, rope, slash. Tight as a knot in binder-twine. Faint hope. Legally bound (not just the feet), "Exclusion Act," head tax, railway car to an internment camp, non-status outskirts of town nomad other side of tracks no track. Mi-nus mark, not equal sign. A shadow, a fragile particle of ash, a residue of ghost bone down the creek without a bridge for the elusive unacknowledged "im" of migratory tongue some cheek to trespass kick the gate the door the either/or, the lottery and the laundry mark, the double mirror, the link between. How float this sign, this agent of the stand-in. Caboose it loose and let it go, it's "Not in Service" anymore. (*Faking It*, p.94–95)

Hyphens are crucial to the composition of *Diamond Grill*, just as doors and their hinges are material to the implicit metaphors of hyphenation and operate as central figures in the book. The book opens in that space so typical of mid-century, small town cafes, the swinging doors between the kitchen and the dining room, between the cooks and the customers, the body and memory (see p.1, "I pick up an order and turn, back through the doors, whap! My foot registers more than its own imprint, starts to read the stain of memory"). And closes, or RE-turns, to another door, the back door (see p.176, "the door clangs and rattles a noisy hyphen between the muffled winter outside and the silence of the warm and waiting kitchen inside").

The hyphen's dynamics, its conceptual profile, its literalness, is provocative of the large question of "inbetweenness". Everything that surrounds our thinking about the hyphen seems suited to my interest in composing language. Its marginalized position (and I don't mean only racially), its noisy—sometimes transparent, sometimes opaque—space feels nurturing. Its coalitional and mediating potentiality offers real engagement, not as a centre but as a provocateur of flux, floating, fleeting. Theresa Cha offers a wonderfully accurate sense in *Dictee*: "You are moving inside. Inside the stillness. Its slowness makes almost imperceptible the movement. Pauses. Pauses hardly rest. New movement, ending only to extend into the next movement" (p.51). The idea of an exterior/interior being connected or separated privileges the extremities; I want that "noisy hyphen" of a door clanging and rattling the measure of such movement. For *Diamond Grill*, and for me, then, the title of this afterword, "Re-Mixed," is a key to both how the text was written as well as why it was written.

A text, a story, a poem, begins again and again. To begin again, I always say to myself as a writer. RE-DO that—again. In hindsight now, I sometimes think I can locate a tangible beginning for *Diamond Grill*. It was in a poem in a book of transcreations (*Pictograms from the Interior of B.C.*, Talonbooks, 1975, p.16) of Indian rock paintings I worked on in the mid-70s.

September spawn
fish weirs everywhere
all through the narrows

Upstream, upstream

A feast for all of us
cousins and old friends
everybody dancing
like crazy, eh?

That word "transcreation" is from Coleridge (*Literary Reminiscences [1839], IV, 166).*

"Not the qualities merely, but the root of the qualities
is transcreated. How else could it be a birth, a creation?"

and that etymon, "trans-", becomes, also, like "cousin", a little burr, another little thorn, that has prodded the discourse of the hyphen for me since "betweenness" also frequently engages a "crossing over," a transcreation, trans-lation, trans-port. The implications of such a term around notions of Diaspora, foreignicity, and multiculturalism are clear (see p.5, YET LAN-GUAGELESS. MOUTH ALWAYS A GAUZE, WORDS LOCKED).

Re-reading that piece now, I recognize the complex of the trans-; the trans-oceanic crossing, the transplanting

"Hi Fred. Just a quick note to tell you that last week I made the tomato beef, and it was wonderful; it's been a wish of mine for a long time to try out some of these recipes, and today I brought the tomato beef into class . . . The students loved it . . . I hid the ginger under my plate."

Cheers, Neil

back and forth of my father and his sister, and then the compositional repetition of that adverb of time—"Yet"—and the resonant rhyming in the run-on sentence still so much a part of our reception of poetry, not prose. Perhaps Coleridge might have said a "re-birth," a "re-creation." Translation can certainly attest to that sense of the RE, the repetition. *Diamond Grill*, as it turned out, is actually the last section of a long poem. During the 70s and 80s, the Canadian Long Poem was central to the drive for local literary identity, particularly the documentary long poem and its utility in inserting local and personal histories into the national imaginary. The long poem compounds itself by tonal iteration. The form uses such devices as repetition of linguistic segments that become narrative by accretion. The novel normally uses narrative differently; it usually shapes a text by delineation and containment. In this biofiction I try to suggest narrative through intertextuality with some of my earlier poems, image and photographic fragments, and clips and anecdotes out of nostalgia and memory. I don't want the narrative to feel too settled and defined or concluded, so, as is characteristic of the long poem, the resistance to closure becomes, in a sense, a resistance to plot and story.

After *Pictograms,* the bio started to demand more in my writing. As a long poem, *Diamond Grill* is really anchored in my next project after *Pictograms,* a collection of poems called *Breathin' My Name With a Sigh*

(Talonbooks, 1981). This was a crucial writing project for me since, around 1979, finally, after twenty years of writing, I was able to confront my racialized past, albeit mostly as an address to my father's death fourteen years earlier. So that other RE, the more nebulous RE of regarding, starts to particularize my own name, Wah. What's that all about, I start to ask. *Breathin' My Name With a Sigh* opens with this poem:

> I like the purity of all things seen
> through the accumulation of thrust
> forward especially the vehicle
> container maybe/or "thing" called body
> because time seems to be only *it* appears
> to look into the green mountains valleys
> or through them to the rivers & nutrient creeks
> *where* was never the problem animal is
> I still have a name "breathin' it
> with a sigh"

This project around naming continues through a couple of books of poetry on into *Diamond Grill* where it, for example, resonates with the later recognition of a childhood interpellation (see p.98, UNTIL MARY MCNUTTER CALLS ME A CHINK I'M).

In 1985 I published a follow-up book to *Breathin' My Name With a Sigh* called *Waiting for Saskatchewan* (Turnstone Press), a series of poems and prose-poems that explore more incisively my rediscovered "Chineseness," in response, no doubt, to the changing racialized times—Joy Kogawa's *Obasan*, Japanese Canadian redress, the move to officialize multiculturalism, and so forth. The title poem situates that narrative I was enmeshed in:

> Waiting for Saskatchewan
> and the origins grandparents countries places converged
> europe asia railroads carpenters nailed grain elevators

Swift Current my grandmother in her house
he built on the street
and him his cafes namely the "Elite" on Center
looked straight ahead Saskatchewan points to it
Erickson Wah Trimble houses train station tracks
arrowed into downtown fine clay dirt prairies wind waiting
for Saskatchewan to appear for me again over the edge
horses led to the huge sky the weight and colour of it
over the mountains as if the mass owed me such appearance
against the hard edge of it sits on my forehead
as the most political place I know these places these strips
laid beyond horizon for eyesight the city so I won't have to go
near it as origin town flatness appears later in my stomach why
why on earth would they land in such a place
mass of Pleistocene
sediment plate wedge
arrow sky beak horizon still waiting for that
I want it back, wait in this snowblown winter night
for that latitude of itself its own largeness
my body to get complete
it still owes me, it does

But the father/racialized hyphen story kept bugging me.

Even the cover photo of *Diamond Grill* shows a fragmented layering of narrative. It's a multiple exposure, a reject, found in my mother's footstool of old family photos. The biofiction, then, is that years later the little boy on the swing must imagine the self, generated by the arms of the loving father and the distant colonial mimicry of the Chinese grandfather, spiffy in his dress-up costume, visage through the haze of migration and hybridity.

Regarding the "MIX" in the title of this afterword, I sense that term could be one of modernism's major vectors to imbed itself in our contemporary social, not only in our national imaginaries but also globally

"I was curious about what you said about the Chinook Jargon and how you always thought the Chinese cooks were swearing at you in Chinese when they said 'you mucka high'. Not too long ago, I used to work in a Chinese restaurant and the guys always used to swear in Chinese. They'd say 'do nigga hi' and 'do mucka hi', very close to 'you mucka high'. I thought it was odd how similar sounding the phrases are. My boss was from Hoiping. I know none of them came until the mid 1980s, so I don't think they learned any Chinook pidgin. Anyways, I found that interesting. You may know this already but . . . when I asked my boss how to say the word for a mixed person he said, 'oh no—you don't want to say that, it's mean', and the Vietnamese word for mixed is also derogatory, but my boyfriend, who is Philippino says there the term (mustesa/o) does not have negative connotations at all, though the term for Muslim is, and they look down on the indigenous peoples there. I wonder why that is. Maybe because the Americans 'rescued' them."

Respectfully, Mercedes

or planetarily (see p.83, I'M JUST A BABY, MAYBE SIX MONTHS [.5%]). At one point I had even thought of titling the book "Mixed Grill" (see p.2).

I take "biofiction" as the sometimes necessary "making up" (even "dressing up") the memory and images of a life, texting the "bio," hence "biotext," the story of the cell(f). As Robert Creeley was once asked, "Was that a real poem, or did you just make it up?" Or another of my teachers, Robert Duncan: "You tell the truth the way the words lie." I think of "biotext" as a means to prevent the kind of writing I do in *Diamond Grill* being hijacked by ready-made generic expectations such as the novel, autobiography, and life writing. As I neared finishing with the text I realized I was using my imagination and opaque memory (my "poetic licence") to embellish and elaborate the stories, so I tinted it as "biofiction." That is, I was able to see the biographical as something constructed, a life made palpable, comprehensible, imaginable. I tried, not so much to tell a story, but to show myself (and others, hopefully) what possible, plausible narrative threads a life can be. I hoped to explain myself to myself. Both as a resistance to the tyranny of fiction, and the predictable forms of narrative such as plot and character, I chose to configure the writing around the form of the anecdote. The anecdote about King's Family Restaurant (see p.136), for example, offers to generate an embellishment of the racialized identity and its frequent position of equivocation and ambivalence (see *Faking It*, p.124).

How to depoeticize the anecdote by claiming its artificiality arises within the poetics of the prose poem and its attention to the expectation of the sentence as a unit of composition. The compounding run-on sentence, ungrammatical frequently, comes not so much from the world of prose as from the world of the prose poem where the tyranny of the "correct" grammatical sentence has been challenged. An extreme example of this in *Diamond Grill* is the long sentence on the Chinese Head Tax (see p.130). That long, compounding sentence is both a nod to the basis of my poetry writing, jazz improvisation, as well as an attempt to dislodge the privilege of the (complete) sentence. The book favours the symbiosis of the serial poem over the narrativity of the novel. The basic unit of composition in *Diamond Grill* is the "anecdote," torqued by the playful syntax of the prose poem and the turn of the cadence in the stanzagraph. Any coherences in the story are due to resonance and iteration. The tropes of the "door" and the "food" have elicited common responses.

The most crucial place for the compounding and/or disjunctive sentence is in the cadence of the paragraph, that kingpin of prose, the finale, the denouement. e.g.:

> Thus: a kind of heterocellular recovery reverberates
> through the busy body, from the foot against that kitchen
> door on up the leg into the torso and hands, eyes thinking
> straight ahead, looking through doors and languages, skin

recalling its own reconnaissance, cooked into the steamy
food, replayed in the folds of elsewhere, always far away,
tunneling through the centre of the earth, mouth saying
can't forget, mouth saying what I want to know can feed
me, what I don't can bleed me. (p.1)

The privileging of the apprehensive potential of language on the move
at the expense of making meaning is important in "compound" composition, in "RE-" poetics, in order to unsettle, paradoxically, the inten-
tion of language to establish meaning. I'm not so much interested, in
this method of composition, in clarity and closure, but in openness and
unpredictability.

The compound compositional approach works also, of course, in
larger segments of the book. Though it's "life writing," there is no sig-
nificant plot. Some of the book occurs on December 21, 1951, but the
temporal here is not so much plot-driven as historically driven. The
cafe is a 50s cafe, which is important for both the history of Chinese–
Canadians as well as for the "I" of the biotext since that time marks
his own "Naming." As I said earlier, vis-à-vis *Breathin' My Name With
a Sigh*, the roots of the process for this particular "long-poem" are in
talking back to one's own name—WAH, the enactment of Althusser's
concept of interpellating the subject, particularly in a racial context (see
p.169, THE NAME'S ALL I'VE HAD TO WORK THROUGH).

In Ashok Mathur's interview with me about *Diamond Grill* I was
asked (in reference to SITKUM DOLLAH GRAMPA WAH, p.68):

"Does being of mixed race (however that's interpreted) create
a kind of shifting race-identification? To put it in different
words, does the mixed-race subject approach a stable racial
identity which can never be reached?"

To which I replied:
Yes and No. In the section SITKUM DOLLAH . . . I try to suggest a gen-

erational transing of the Chinook term "high muckamuck," from its origins through my grandfather, father and mother. Racialized spaces in my family seem to have occurred similarly. That is, my grandfather likely didn't have to be a "chink" until he was called one. My father, being of mixed race, was undoubtedly more familiar with the instability, the shifting, of racial identity as he was racially slurred in China and in Canada. I'm sure he desired a more stable racial space (don't we all) but had witnessed the destabilization of sure identities throughout his life, particularly in the descriptive containment of the Chinese in Canada. The racialized space certainly seems to me to be specific to history and person. Race, in North America, can be modified, to a degree, through class. This is even more possible for a mixed-race person (portrayed nicely in James Weldon Johnson's *Autobiography of an Ex-Colored Man*). The reality of the formula, though, is surely the whiter you are the more class you have. So no, identity is never pure, never sure. And in that the hybrid has as much possibility of "a" sure racial identity as anyone; the only thing sure about it, however, is, as you suggest, that it's always shifting. The sureness of shifting. Thanks to Mary McNutter, I not only know who she thinks I am but I know immediately the space she has cleared for both of us is exclusive, surprising, and volatile.

Much of my "thinking" behind and around *Diamond Grill* can be located in my subsequent book *Faking It: Poetics and Hybridity*, NeWest Press, 2000. In fact, I included in *Faking It*, besides Ashok Mathur's informative interview with me about *Diamond Grill*, an anecdote that was supposed to be in *Diamond Grill* but somehow got lost (in "Half-Bred Poetics," *Faking It*, p.76–78). Given this second chance, I include it here.

(Vancouver, British Columbia, 1963)

Hello, is this the U.S. consulate? I'm calling about getting a visa. I'm going to Albuquerque as a graduate student but I'd like to be able to work in the States.

What's your name?

Wah. Double U, Ay, Aych. Fred Wah.

Is that a Chinese name?

Yes it is. Why?

I'm afraid you'll have to apply under the Asian quota, sir, and there's a backup of several-years' on the Asian list.

But I'm a Canadian.

I'm afraid that doesn't matter. If you're of Chinese origin, even if you're born in Canada, you still have to go under the Asian quota.

Well that's ridiculous. Could I come down and talk to the Consul General about this?

By all means, but he's a busy . . .

I'll be right down.

(fast over False Creek down Burrard to Georgia—down-town)

And what can I do for you, sir?

My name's Fred Wah. I talked with the receptionist on the

phone this morning about getting a visa. She told me that, even though I'm Canadian, because my racial origin is Chinese, I'll have to apply under the Asian quota.

But you don't look Chinese.

That's because I'm half Swedish. I'm only quarter Chinese.

Well, that makes all the difference then. If you're less than fifty percent you can enter the U.S. as a Canadian. Just ask the girl out front for the forms, it shouldn't take more than a few days.

You had me fooled there.

SOME USEFUL REFERENCES:

Cabri, Louis. "'Diminishing the Lyric I': Notes on Fred Wah & the Social Lyric." *Open Letter* 12.3 (Fall 2004): 77–91.

Day, Iyko. "Interventing Innocence: Race, 'Resistance,' and the Asian North American Avant-Garde." *Literary Gestures: The Aesthetic in Asian American Writing*, edited by Rocío G. Davis and Sue-Im Lee. Temple University Press, 2005.

Derksen, Jeff. "Making Race Opaque: Fred Wah's Poetics of Opposition and Differentiation." *West Coast Line* 17, 29.3 (Winter 1995-96): 63–76.

Kamboureli, Smaro. "Faking it: Fred Wah and the postcolonial imaginary." *Études Canadiennes/Canadian Studies: revue interdisciplinaire des études Canadiennes en France (Assn Française d'Études Canadiennes, Talence)* 54 (2003): 115–32.

McGonegal, Julie. "Hyphenating the Hybrid 'I': (Re)Visions of Racial Mixedness in Fred Wah's *Diamond Grill*." *Essays in Canadian Writing* 75 (Winter 2002): 177–95.

Rudy, Susan. "Hybridity and Asianicity in Canada." Interview. *Poet's Talk*, Pauline Butling and Susan Rudy, University of Alberta Press, 2005: 143–169.

Saul, Joanne. "Displacement and self-representation: theorizing contemporary Canadian biotexts." *Biography: An Interdisciplinary Quarterly,* 24:1 (2001): 259–72.

Sugars, Cynthia. "'The negative capability of camouflage': fleeing Diaspora in Fred Wah's *Diamond Grill*." *Studies in Canadian Literature* 26:1 (2001): 27.

Faking It: Poetics & Hybridity
The Writer as Critic Series: VII

According to Fred Wah, the act of thinking critically is one of explora-
tion and discovery. In *Faking It*, Wah demonstrates how writing poetry is
writing critically. This scrapbook of Wah's work—collected from fifteen
years of his writing—contains essays, reviews, journals, notes and, most
importantly, poetic improvisations on contemporary poetry and identity.
Faking It was written between 1984 and 1999—during major shifts in
critical thinking and cultural production—and the hybrid style of the
book is an apt reflection of these changing times, as well as a reflection
and study of Wah's own hybrid identity.

ISBN 10: 1-896300-07-3 / ISBN 13: 978-1-896300-07-8
$24.95 CDN / $19.95 US
Trade Paperback / 280 PP / Available Now